the *religious* *mantle*

NUNO JÚDICE

the religious mantle

Translated from Portuguese by
David Swartz

All rights reserved. Published by New Meridian, part of the non-profit organization New Meridian Arts, 2020.

LIBRARY OF CONGRESS CATALOGING-IN-PUBLICATION DATA

The Religious Mantle
Authored by Nuno Júdice

ISBN: 978-1-7343835-1-5
LCCN: 2020935761

Support for the translation and publication of this project was generously provided by the Portuguese Republic through *Direção-Geral do Livro, dos Arquivos e das Bibliotecas.*

REPÚBLICA PORTUGUESA

CULTURA
DIREÇÃO-GERAL DO LIVRO, DOS ARQUIVOS E
DAS BIBLIOTECAS

Acknolwedgements

I WOULD LIKE TO THANK my wife Carla Magalhães for her invaluable help revising the manuscript at its earliest stages, Nava Renek for her interest, commitment and confidence in this project and for her tireless support in preparing the text for publication, Alexandru Oprescu for his superb work arranging and designing the book and Nuno Júdice for making himself available to read and respond to my translation throughout its various stages of revision.

Introduction

"THE WORK OF NUNO JÚDICE IS LIKE A SPELL,"
Millicent Borges Accardi once wrote in the *Por-
tuguese-American Journal*. "A reverie. A dark dream
with quiet overtones and hidden meanings." She
was speaking of his poetry, but the same could be
said for *The Religious Mantle*, Júdice's novella, which
came out in 1982 as *A Manta Religiosa,* and is published here for the first time in an English translation
by David Swartz.

As if playing Virgil to his own Dante, the narrator of *The Religious Mantle* spins a labyrinthine inner
dialogue, which at times approaches an *ars poetica*,
a meditation on the poetic novel. In fact, the entire
novella is written in the form of a dialogue between
two male characters who are projections of the "I."
Together, they are "somewhat like the heteronyms of
Pessoa," as Júdice explained to me in an email.

While the male characters are fluid, less grounded
and fleshed-out, the three female characters—
Paula, Raquel, and Clara—represent distinct female
archetypes. Clara, like Dante's Beatrice is the more

ephemeral of the three, inaccessible and unattainable; whereas Paula and Raquel are more corporeal.

For the reader, it's often difficult to distinguish between the male characters; who are almost Janus-like in their presentation, representing two sides of one man. And, while we get a physical sense of Paula and Raquel and their presence is real, Clara looms over the pages of the novella like a unreachable ideal. We feel for the narrator, who can't keep his mind off Clara. (And we feel not a little sorry for Paula, who sometimes seems caught in the middle between the narrator and his unachievable desires.)

～

Nuno Júdice was born in Mexilhoeira Grande, in the Algarve, the southernmost region of continental Portugal. He is a Professor of Literature at the Universidade Nova in Lisbon and currently serves as editor of the Gulbenkian Foundation literary magazine, *Colóquio-Letras*. He published his first poetry book in 1972, *A Noção de Poema,* which translates as "The Notion of Poem," followed by many others, and he has been the recipient of several renowned poetry prizes. Throughout the years, he has also published extensively as a fiction writer, an essayist, and a literary critic.

I first met Júdice in 1994, during his only trip to the United States. He gave a reading at Poets House in New York along with another Portuguese poet,

Pedro Tamem, and the translator Richard Zenith. I had recently begun to explore my own Portuguese heritage—two of my maternal great-grandparents emigrated from the Azores in 1906 and I've since traced my Portuguese roots to 1402 in the Alentejo—and hearing Júdice and Tamem read from their work in the mesmerizing and sometimes confounding language of my ancestors was an intoxicating experience. These were my first contemporary Portuguese poets—I'd read Camões and Pessoa in translation—and they read in a language that seemed as ancient to me as it proved difficult to learn.

In August 2018, my wife Samantha and I had dinner with Júdice while we were in Lisbon. We met at the old bull-fighting ring that has been turned into a mall, Praça de Touros, in a bookstore located in the basement. His books were on display and I recall he bought a couple of copies of one title because he'd run out. He took us back to his apartment in Campo Pequeno and, as expected, it was filled with books and art, much by artists he's known. His study provided further evidence that this was the home of a poet and professor: stacks of books and papers, dark wood paneling, and bookshelves on all sides.

Driving out along the coast west of Lisbon, he took us to a favorite restaurant in Cascais. The restaurant owner greeted the poet like an old friend and sat us at a table by a window. We had a lovely meal, talking about poetry and the current state of

Portuguese and American writing, and about what we'd seen in Lisbon, Porto, and the Azores. During the return drive, Júdice regaled us with notable tales of the coastal area—Cascais was the traditional summer retreat of the Portuguese nobility—and provided us a history lesson about the time of the Carnation Revolution and immediately after.

At the end of the evening, Júdice graciously dropped us off near the entrance to the neighborhood where we were staying. He was heading for his house in the Algarve the next morning. As soon as he drove off, I realized I'd left my phone in his car. I turned, but he was gone. We made our way as quickly as possible to the apartment we'd rented and I fired up my laptop, sending him a desperate email. He found my phone and, as it was now late in the evening, we agreed to meet the next morning at the Gulbenkian Foundation. We planned to the see an exhibition there that day—art from around the time of the revolution in the 1970s—we had a coffee and Júdice had his associates let us into the exhibit while he bid us adieu. The show provided insight into the Portuguese resistance during an important time of the poet's youth.

As a student in university during the protests in 1968, Júdice witnessed first-hand the early stages of the revolution and, although not explicitly called out in the novella, this era serves as a backdrop for *The Religious Mantle*, as it did more overtly in his book, *Plankton,* which precedes it. These were the years leading up to 1974's Carnation Revolution, the peaceful military coup that overthrew the authoritarian Estado Novo regime. This period of growing dissatisfaction of youth under the Salazar dictatorship, and frustration with Portugal's Colonial Wars in Africa, fomented a distrust among what Júdice calls a "lost generation"—lost from the repression preventing freedoms they knew existed in more democratic countries. It's in this context that *The Religious Mantle* should be read—although contemporary readers in the United States without such context may be familiar enough with the sense of the narrator's discomfort and a certain oppressive paranoia that lingers throughout the book.

❦

Laura Miller, writing in the *New Yorker*, once described the stereotypical "poet's novel" as being "introspective, replete with long passages of description, and scant of plot." Indeed, Júdice's novella is no exception to that description. Not much *happens* in the novella; it is decidedly not plot-driven, rather, it's more a work of philosophical discursiveness.

In fact, much of the "action" of *The Religious Mantle* is the narrator-writer searching for his form. As critic Maria Estela Guedes wrote at the time of its Portuguese release, "Notes, dialogues with embryonic characters, diary entries, poetic segments, narrative sketches, which, as stated elsewhere in the book, constitute the material with which the author-character could organize a novel."

Júdice himself confirmed this impression, writing to me that he still finds the book, a little intriguing: "Now that I reread it, I begin to find a narrative logic, given by the passages in italics that show the evolution of the narrator's state of mind throughout the book."

Philosophical and discursive novels are a style that have—sadly, in my humble opinion—gone out of style. While *The Religious Mantle* is as much a book of philosophy as it is a book of fiction, with its search for meaning from within a labyrinth of feelings and ideas, one never feels one is reading an artifact, and translator David Swartz deftly manages to make the novella sound contemporary and fresh.

In this and other works of fiction, Júdice is part of a long Portuguese tradition of poets writing prose, starting with Almeida Garrett and Alexandre Herculano, in the 19th Century, and extending through Pessoa to Miguel Torga, José Rego, Vitorino Nemésio, Jorge de Sena, David Mourão-Ferreira, Natália Correia, Maria Judite de Carvalho, Olga Gonçalves, Carlos de Oliveira, and Adelaide Freitas.

American poet and novelist, April Bernard, once said, "fiction is a mess and poetry is a dance." Júdice, for his part, agrees with this sentiment. "For me, poetry is rigor and precision of the word," he wrote to me. "Fiction begins by being chaotic and only in the course of writing do I begin to find an order that will lead to the final book."

～

Portuguese literature needs more translation into English—in support of this statement, I offer the list of poets and prose writers above: how many did you recognize? It is time to go beyond Pessoa, José Saramago, and António Lobo Atunes—as worthy as they are—to bring to light the rich tradition of Portugal's "lost generation," and those writing since. Outside of the 2012 selection published as *The Cartography of Being*, selected and translated by Paulo da Costa, and what can be found on a couple of websites, Júdice's work, and the work of his contemporaries, is very little known to readers of English.

David Swartz's translation of *The Religious Mantle* is a valuable contribution that sheds light on the work of an important writer. One hopes this heralds a new age of discovery for the Portuguese; an age that leads with works rather than deeds, with literature rather than colonization.

—*SCOTT EDWARD ANDERSON*

*S*tone houses, fishing boats in the cove, a tavern with a wide entrance, the full cold autumn sun, old wooden tables. I enter and sit down on a bench. I'm exhausted. I say it out loud to believe it. The tavern keeper laughs. He sits down in front of me. "Waiting for the winter? The dirty hole of generations? Is it fear?" Yes, I was beginning to age. I didn't have grey hair, but I slept badly, dreams had ceased to follow a logical pattern; there was a sense of obscurity. Would you like me to continue? Shall I tell you about how I lost a friend following a literary discussion? I defended the idea that creation is not possible within a style. The writer's role is to arrange already invented letters and words inside the space of a blank page. A sudden squawk of seabirds diverted my attention. I go out to the stone porch and feel with difficulty the sunshine on my face, eyes half-closed. A mouse hole is the end. I feel myself descending inwards until I reach the bottom of a circular pit, my hands searching along the top ledge for my soul. The sea is a grey puddle in this place. A fishing village. I am looking for a sailor's cap in my memory. The anchor. A blue visor. I wander up and down the main drag in search of the fugitive image. I arrive at dusk. The autumn sky is filled with vast clouds threatening rain. And if I hid under the trees? Or inside the roots? Or if, eager for moisture, I descended underground, into apparent immobility, extending my arms in search of water? I feel a tap on my back. "How long has it been since you came here? Listen: do you know about the lagoon? The smell of the swamp at

*low tide? The clouds of mosquitoes at night? The song of
the insane mermaid? For two years a novelist lived there.
He came to my house regularly to buy candles, matches,
ink, the old Parker Quink. He doesn't even need to speak.
I give him these things willingly, which he puts in an old
bag. I tell him a couple of stories, mainly rumors and
dirty anecdotes. A man only needs the obscenity of others.
But he's only interested in time. For two years he's lived
there, and still hasn't learned to interpret the connection
between the changes in the seasons and the activities of
birds; the variations of colors in the water; the noise of
the wind through the reeds and bushes on the margins.
Elementary things."*

1

Momentarily liberated from my obsessions, I sat down at a cafe to design a plan of cosmic organization such as the mystics had only suspected. I was engaged in this work when an individual of indeterminate age appeared before me.

—I bring the image of a city by the sea, where the flight of seagulls are confounded by caesuras: one after the other, rising up from the waves, they reach the land.

I remained gazing at him without saying anything. A sickness came over my spirit, forcing me to lower my eyes to the height of a chair. I found myself on the ground, breathing in the dust, when suddenly dogs came rushing towards me, quarreling over my body.

—They had broken the stained-glass windows. At night, one could see the outlines of the mountains through narrow spaces, trees agitated in the unquiet blackness, inclining their tops like twisted shoulders without heads. Inside the church I heard the wind howling over the rooftops and up through the tower. The morning set itself apart. The sensation of entering into immense night. The remaining light had disappeared into vacuous pockets of memory. I leaned myself up against the wall. My hands touched the humid plaster, the moss entered into a cavity that opened into empty compartments, the sound of a mad siren came over me.

He interrupted me:

—Tie me to the mast! I demand it.

—From the lips, blood runs to the fingers, down to the knees. Divine work rots us.

I knew he had followed me chronicling my every gesture and action. He showed me the result—a simple scheme, which, since then, has served to systematize my existence by varying the criteria for moral judgements between good and evil.

—Screaming and crying like a newborn child, I extend my arms along the wall, preventing myself from returning to a more primitive form. Can the sunset keep me from being a child? From suffering like the sick? From harboring poisonous memories? I knew that I had no hope of answering. Night, the devouring abyss, sleep, the passage to the luminous world. The tunnel, the legions of spirits.

—The world engenders the monsters of reason. Reason opens its legs for people to drink its sick blood…I was already on my feet. I paid up and left for the square. A streetcar passed, screeching along the tracks. This noise in my head remained, and hours later, in the boat, I tried to reproduce it with my teeth. At that time, I was vulnerable to the sounds of reality. The beating of the hull against the water, the bird-songs, the voice of women, these things called to me and diverted my attention from the abstract profundity of existence. I searched for the Poet and told him I was returning to the country. Each time dusk arrived, I looked towards the horizon, faintly remembering the final flicker of twilight. I discovered that I saw everything distinctly. I could discern which were the fundamental colors of the sky and describe the relative disposition of the clouds and hills and their mutations.

He stood for austerity: "I could move towards excess, exhaust myself, but my education, the difficulties of childhood…the lock in time, prevented me from attaining such pleasure." The same was happening to his writings. His texts had a moderate, balanced tone. He distrusted baroque ornamentation and superficiality. This frugal kind of language was attractive to his generation, yet few appreciated his work. At times one or another reaction arose, perhaps unexpectedly, but without failing to unnerve him: "Why do people read my writing? I know that I have nothing to say, that there is no use in waiting for some kind of revelation from me. And even so, people look for me!" He said this without modesty, with conviction, but inside this conviction lay the weakness of his argument. He needed people to believe in him; only a few had the audacity to do so.

One day he was seized with a sudden impulse to create: to write a novel. He filled a notebook with scattered notes, the majority of which were autobiographical. He knew not what would come of it. But at last he set himself apart from poetry. The concise mode, the emotional concentration, the dominant feeling, disappeared from his style. The sentence was lengthened and lost its musicality. Had it begun to "grow?" To acquire the maturity one spoke of as being the supreme virtue?

"It was then," he wrote, "that the narrative became fragmented, and it is possible that its objective detached itself, dispersing into sporadic, errant directions. This did not mean that his point of departure was not correct, or that the influence of the elements of Reason had not determined his hesitation and previous gestures. The despair which was supposed to be part of his work wasn't understood; the presence and function of his characters remained obscure, as did the situation relative to the author's materiality and voice. But if all this points out real defects, here, there are no explanations, nor coincidences. Only fragmentation is real since truth itself is dispersive. It is because of this that nothing is certain, for if anything were certain there would be no need to begin from the beginning."

—Nothing is sufficiently impossible. I live and I dream. Sensations stream. Slowly I lose my intellectual dimension. I run away from reason, from exact and material existence.

He finished writing, settled the paper on top of the table, rose to his feet, and began to walk across the terrace in no particular direction, looking out at the sea. I remembered what he had told me.

—It was this: illumination appears suddenly. The celestial fire, the wings of an angel brushing up against the back of one's hands, leaving behind an impression of marked sublimity. With aerial effulgence one's eyes say farewell to human light, muddying the walls with the vertiginous shadow of madness.

A single page was already excessive for him. He limited himself to half a dozen lines, often written without any concern for making sense. He conjoined words only to fill space on the page. Without order or chronology, each sheet would be arbitrarily assembled together. From this collage of disconnected elements, the text randomly emerged. "The true order is chaos itself," he said.

His first book developed from this series of improvisations. He had been accumulating texts, adding them one to the other. In the end, he changed only the narration from first to third person, giving the text a fluency which he found surprising. He never thought he would be capable of inventing figures and arguments. He had always lived at the margins of a story. He had lost successive opportunities. His dramatic situations were "fictional"—what others had already written—and it left him without a subject.

Now, suddenly, he considered himself to be this vast material to be treated. An unexpected sense of subterranean energy and interior logic. He discovered a capacity to intervene in things that surrounded him, to reach people emotionally, whom he had always ignored.

—I know today that certain creative processes are not compatible with life. Genius is renunciation, the final dismissal of everything dirty about human existence. I am able to say that I saw the divine in its lower forms; but beyond that, did I have the initiative required to make the journey? I knew about the fraternity of obscure and ruined churches; there, where the corrosion of time had realized clear lines of construction, pure shadows and still-visible arches. Meditation dragged me into its infernal flow. The afternoon enveloped me with the tepid protection of clarity, and I lost myself in the abyss.

Thus began our mutual relationship, and in a short time I surrendered myself to the confused intricacy of sentiment in which, as actors, we disperse ourselves. Today, however, I see that my objective was not reduced to one individual perception, but had society as a target, and the general climate of the times.

—A neo-renaissance.

—I was born to write; I write to be reborn.

To enter into this phase of paradox he became deranged and pulled out the chair from behind him, creating an absurd space between his body and the table. His right hand, which, at the beginning had only made some gestures outlining one or another word, now moved rapidly, tapping me on the shoulder, stroking the furniture, pointing to the wall and to the door.

—To life!

I went out of the cafe disoriented, lightheaded. Some years ago, not yet having reached the age to have had experienced an interior vision, I was too much a prisoner of my contradictions to be able to change myself. Now, however, I chose a different path. My face indicated a soul tortured by doubt and multiple spiritual conflicts. Under these circumstances I met Clara. We talked about others because we knew nothing about ourselves. Sometimes we would go to the outskirts of town in search of winter's forgotten interior, only to have my suspicions confirmed that everything happens randomly due to the pure deviation of nature. One night, in front of the sea, I saw tears running down her face. The shadows disappeared. From another perspective, she told me it was the shadow itself taking possession of the opaque and immobile bodies.

At that time, I made innumerable attempts to write, but lacked a scheme, an organizing principle. One day I came across an old professor.

—I trusted you. You were one of the few from whom I expected a work, a recognizable name. But you haven't given proof of what you're capable of. What are you waiting for?

I kept silent. I was afraid to say that I had given up writing—which did not entirely correspond to the truth, but I also didn't dare reveal my occult activities, the incessant search for a form beyond form. After all, to what purpose had the masters served me? From some of them I learned the requirements of maintaining a certain pose, the simple attitude before the circumstance; from others I understood the compromise one makes with the most sordid aspects of life's journey. In succeeding generations, they acted like a dyke made of sand waiting for the seismic wave that would sweep them up, repeating words and gestures, rousing reactions which they hoped would be identical year after year—to confirm their theory of the degradation of the species. There was a lack of ideas, of ideals; or was it rather the curse of the climate, the sterility of the land? The masters had suffered from excess of confidence—and now paid dearly for holding on to this illusion.

The Poet himself could no longer hear me. What thought had he given to publishing a book? He understood poetry as something minor. His objective was a novel: to transcribe an epoch in its profoundest most essential aspects, leaving aside surface sentiment, vain emotional agitation. Meanwhile, he prepared a study on the mechanics of coastal birds, while I wandered without courage, repeating to myself the same phrases adopted from old platitudes.

—I think he's "androgynous." Clara said about the Poet. I didn't need to distrust anything. I collected elements, laughing to myself.

—From the window I could see the railway tracks, and every dawn I would wake up to the sound of wind or to the noisy screeching of old locomotives coming from the North. There, I didn't worry about my individual existence, or the occasional dramas that swirled around me.

She insulted me: "Egoist!"

—At the end, I returned without having obtained wisdom, but gained some new understanding of the soul and of people.

My ambition was to demand aesthetics from all of my efforts. But when I arrived at the point of making this proposal, I didn't speak. With my hand, I wiped away the sweat running down my forehead; and in a gesture of self-sacrifice, I compressed my stomach.

—You want to create a Poetic Character. I condemn you to failure, the Poet repeated.

In reality, I was trying to imitate the Apostate. He appeared every night with his indeterminate age and his smell of aguardente. People laughed at him. They couldn't understand his deeply nocturnal nature. Perhaps they thought that everything ought to be integrated into the normal passage of time and the specific transformations of the species.

—He kept silent for many moments. Then I saw him. He had taken up an attitude of extreme studious rigor, searching for obscure definitions that neither he nor anybody else could clarify. Nor was he making an effort. He talked in a syncopated manner, searching for rhythm but not meaning. As a result, his sentences appeared to derive from momentary inspiration, in a way that made it difficult to follow his reasoning—presupposing that reason was there at all. He transformed himself, his eyes turning from a blueish color to a confused grey, whereupon they gazed at the stagnant pond, the grasses, the slime, the fish in the river, the fertile mud of eternity. I sometimes tried to describe him. He was the ideal character for a novel, or earlier, for a poem—embodying the indefinable and vague tone that doesn't propitiate developments nor conclusions.

—Poetic, yes!

—The texts he composed on dirty sheets of paper and foil revealed the fluency of rapid writing. An elaborate style, the autodidactic knowledge of essential truths, the search for revelation. I knew, meanwhile, that he had prepared a work related to death: not to death in the abstract, but to his own death.

—I want your assistance in my final moment, he told me with a hypocritical smile.

During that time we experienced tense relations because of Clara. One night, drawing close to me, he said:

—I will spend the best of my time contemplating her face, drowning in the smell of aguardente.

I grabbed his arm that had passed over my shoulder, and he fell to the ground. Since that day, he stopped speaking to me about his work, except through indirect allusions, and I lost all conviction in the vague conclusions he appeared to have arrived at. I knew, however, that he sought to make them work for him conjunctively, melting together his delirious imagination with philosophical speculation. The idea that he could predict the future mutations of human beings approached the realm of religious mysticism. He had the appearance of someone who didn't need others anymore. He started to defend dis-humanity: an ideology of solitude, haughtiness, maturity without social firmness, earned only through the hermetic learning of the knowledge of being.

—Nature appears mystical, but the progression of knowledge is not confined to daily life, it appears in certain moments of the "personality," in the formation of a common body, recognizable, and identifiable by a behavior grafted onto the primitive essence of its body—such unexpected reactions I call pure creation.

At last, before the naked walls, he murmured curses and profanities.

—At the end of time you will hear me, he said, and perhaps he spoke the truth. One of his theories concerned the concentric movement of the voice, rising from sphere to sphere in temporal succession as it approached the center.

—Reality is motionless. Beginning from this fundamental principle, I moved towards an understanding of the world. I shall better explain the reasons that persuaded me to first refuse the idea of reality, and secondly, the immobility of truth. The idea that Reality is motionless forces me to seek its ultimate cause in the beginning or end of truth's immobility; and yet, since reality is considered to be both the cause of itself and to depart from the substantiation of that cause, in that which is real I find a double affirmation of Reality. It is something stuck, unable to move, and hence, bearing upon itself with its own weight, gyrating abstractly in its vacuous turning of itself upon its own axis, alone before me, this cause—would present its own justification—that which makes me the true motor of the real. Meanwhile, if I reproduce this game of mirrors ad infinitum, I will be unable to fix myself to a unique point of view, while if I am to find myself fixed, I'd find myself in the place of God, setting myself in His ways.

The words resisted the advance of the imagination, preventing him from thinking and writing as a living person. He abandoned the reflexive style for the dispersion of short phrases—useless and Baroque. This increased his suffering. Being conscious of not advancing, of not progressing in understanding in his search for the absolute, began to oppress him, preventing him from going to the window, or breathing more forcefully. Attempts to free himself would alleviate his sensation of immobility. In these instances, he entered into an abstract dimension of being. Society, memories, culture, family, friends, all vanished. He stood inert, absorbed in the vague image of passed encounters, of which he only remembered the silence, the fatigue. Soon, he returned to life, only to dive back into himself once again, as into a well, without seeing anything, completely drowned, his limbs stuck in the mud.

Besides that, I told him, these ideas do not resolve your disquiet.

I crossed the river, sat down at a table in the cafe and began writing an interpretive sketch of the Real on a large sheet of paper. It was in vain. The almost imperceptible noise of smoke from the cigarette pointing out from the corner of his mouth caused him to feel a profound sorrow for the human condition and made him even more insistently affirm his committment to no longer be compassionate. A sudden impulse, a desire for destruction came over his spirit, forcing him to throw himself to the ground and gnaw the tip of the carpet filthy with ashes, mud, and phlegm. A group of men dragged him into the street, leaning him up against the skeleton of a ship. When the tide breached his feet, he stared at it with an idiotic expression, as if nothing was happening to him. In truth, he was no longer in possession of his own body, and in that terrifying state of anxiety brought on by liberation, he contorted his fingers and eyes, and his lips directed words of doubt and blasphemy towards the succession of beings that came towards him.

—Let the spirit of prose illuminate me! Behind the wheel, Paula remained indifferent to the screaming. The car came to a stop where the pavement ended over the hill. Paula was crying. She took my hands.

—Life is a river. I love you. But what if we were to die?

Her voice came to me filtered through the night's humidity. There were lights in the distance, and we could hear the vague noises of humanity.

—Let's go back.

As we returned to the house, Paula asked if we could forget the tears, the words. When we entered the room, there was singing and dancing. It was a ritual. She felt uncomfortable amongst strangers.

—At the very least, the Poet was there, the hypocrite!

I left her and went to speak with Rachel. She was drunk, her eyes half-opened. She had fallen in love with a woman. The revelation of her secret life preoccupied her now above all else.

—When I first fell in love, at the age of fifteen, I felt nothing. I feel nothing in my life.

She would continue:

—I'd just as soon live than die.

What intrigued me about her was her total igno-rance of literature. There was an obscure sincerity in her words that made me realize, for the first time, the abstract form of my disease. I pulled her towards me, beckoning her to dance, pressing her up against my body. She resisted. Despite her having been drinking, she was pale. I learned later that she wrote poems. But that did not change my opinion. She was too human for talent to corrupt her.

Paula returned to the living room to tell me she was leaving. I decided to stay. My concern consisted of achieving a privileged moment of repose, an appar-ent inactivity of emotion. An analysis of that moment filled me with self-consciousness.

—Today's world, with its apparent dichotomies and contradictions, has opened the door to trivializa-tion. I will transpose it without prejudice. The root of the phenomena resembles the square root of the Divine; the historical result is Man.

People continued to dance in the room. I crossed the backyard and entered the garage where drinks were being served.

—The abstract process of operations (in num-bers) becoming concrete (bodies and inorganic matter) is simple. But we haven't yet mastered it; and that's why, in the end, Man cannot appropriate Chaos.

—I return to simplicity! The sea voyage to the island.

It was the Poet. He had been there getting drunk alone, with a notebook in front of him. At times he laughed.

—What audacity! The Poet composes delirious caprice, joins vital propulsions of the flesh, and prefers Christian morality to natural morality.

—I remembered August: how the wind shook the trees and awnings with the sound of dry crackling, filling my life with sand.

—Men complain about their own experience, accusing it of misleading them; judges subtle in their own reasoning…irreparable errors, multiple lies. The symbol is indubitable, the analogy is evident. It was a mistake! A mistake! Don't give in to the easy appeal of the image, to exuberance and depression, interior enchantment, music, melancholy or madness.

Sitting by the window in the bedroom I could see the boats in the harbor waiting to go out to sea. This expectation encouraged a craving for destruction that has disturbed me ever since, especially during the night, preventing me from sleeping. Wakefulness and insomnia brought nightmares and apocalyptic visions—fixed irreparable images of gigantic convulsions.

—We're not in the world to be loved. Love is nothing but a particular complication within human relationships; it is not required by the act of living. Our first cry is already against love.

Several times I tried to write about what was happening to me. I've never come up with more than fragments, too literary for my purpose. While I persisted in thinking that much later I would put them together in a book, I ceased concerning myself with my own memory.

—The terrestrial paradise banished its melancholy and gave way to the great adventure of love.

He looked at me stunned. The logical conclusion of this series of postulates was already formed in my head: "Only love can guarantee freedom. To love oneself is to cultivate the image of our perpetual re-creation. Love of one's neighbor is the result of the confidence that our own self-love merits." But I had let Paula leave. She had no more arguments.

—God knows the rare perfection of the illegitimate. In Seville I heard all the bells of the city ring at the same time. It was an evening of war.

—I knew such usual manifestations of the romantic spirit, under the ornamental vaults of the word, when memory becomes a glacier descending from the North to influence the likely inhabitants of the poem.

Apparently, I was immobile. During these moments life became literary, the space around me populated by unreal beings, creatures animated by irrationality and fantasy.

—The erotic multiplication of the proofs of sufficiency, essential rumors in the physical spectrum of the soul, announced an intense daily intelligence.

Disorder was a blank piece of paper. There was a possible answer to all questions. The Absolute

Sentence, devouring doubt, partially revealed itself to me each time a verbal image occurred to my spirit.

—I will try to define what it means to be human.

The difficulty of specifying sensitive assumptions about truth led me to silence. The poet suspected that this mystery was nothing more than my own possible truth, or what I could *reveal* about it—a concept whose full scope I do not fully comprehend, and further, which I had already explicitly alluded to as a 'process,' a form of writing which allows one to assume that any explication or explanation wouldn't be more than a technical exercise, placing the fundamental aspects of the creative act in the irremediable shadow of things that, resignedly, we know to be incomprehensible.

—The problem of genius in its relation to everyday things…

To speak of the creative act, in the face of its irony, would be useless, a practice harmful to my physical existence. I answered him:

—I'd rather talk about death.

The words amounted to the image becoming a humid print of the soul, or its very suggestion.

—It rains (as if one were sketching an outline of the landscape, or perhaps a landscape and the minuscule examination of every detail).

A car entered the open gate, and with headlights blaring high, stopped at the door of the garage. It was the Apostate. He came out and started vomiting into a flowerbed. I put on a record. He came in with his thick lips, sat down, lit a cigarette, unbuckled his belt and took out his penis.

—They were dynamos of Sensibility, continued the Poet, flaming conductors sparked by the high emotions brought on by omens… Bringing to the lips the auspices of a feverish country. Dominating the north winds and mild voices of women. They dared not say: "Behold our Kingdom approaches!" They concealed themselves.

The Apostate was pissing.

—I don't know if it's a favorable season for me, he said, in a voice hoarse from effort.

Clouds chasing the horizon made the exercise of divination, transmitted from generation to generation in indecisive volumes of solitary chronicles, difficult to perform.

—I let my soul's Pride obscure my face; I questioned the closed entrails of a sterile land; I heard threatening omens. It was almost morning. A fresh and humid wind arose, bringing with it the smell of the sea, and every half hour, the noise of trains. While many people had already left, those who stayed behind were kissing on the sofas in the living room in the dawn's early light. Rachel entered.

—I'm going to sleep.

—Can I join you?

It was the Apostate. Vomiting had returned him to clarity and manliness. He put his penis back in his pants, piss still smoking at his feet.

—The way to happiness is the way to Power. Temperament is molded in the strenuous forms of perseverance. Ethics and the moral pressures that force one to obey and suffer in silence ought to be abolished; excessive effort is required by the struggle; poverty or the permanence of a lack that cannot be fulfilled—will result in severe pitfalls along the march of progress. Any future confrontation will be an aesthetic definition.

Rachel and the Apostate danced. They also kissed. She abandoned herself with the air of a sleep-walking victim offered up in sacrifice. Much later, in self-justification: "I refused to retreat in the face of the inconvenient accessories of physical resistance. The world was stunned. I defended Unity."

—But can you justify the suffering of others with your own suffering?

—I reacted against disorder and poverty. All optimism appeared to me to be devoid of a basis. I refused options and commitments.

I went out to the garden that was filled with the smell of the night together with the smell of vomit. The Poet followed after me:

—I reinvented the word and the alphabet, which placed me in the humble role of a cultivator of careful research, an artisan of doubt.

A knot of memories. I calmed down. The old images were restoring my ruined spirit. Rachel and the Apostate—would they make love? I recomposed myself. To be at peace with myself I no longer needed grand sentences, nor even people. I would close my eyes, and the past would come over me. In the distance, there was still music, and that would comfort me; it was part of the ritual. I lit a cigarette. The darkness provided me with the necessary environment for my reunion.

—The contemplative force absorbs the will power of the lonely exiles. Wisdom will coincide with the recovery of past triumphs, the auguries of Joy, and the faculty of forgetting will be transformed through each name in history—sublimated in the urgency for silence, nostalgic rumor of a mask unveiled.

—Personal destiny does not exist. I look for the asylum of the Body.

To search for a refuge, or rather to trade the idea of searching for intense impressions and subtle sounds, for the vertigo of refusal. Thus, to gain isolation, the height ("—Oh that unusual ideal! The future life you promised!" laughed Paula...).

With these words I not only discover a nostalgia for the past but saw more deeply into my current life. By removing myself from love, I suddenly lost my soul. I gave myself up to idleness, expecting a future metamorphosis.

—The contemplative force...I repeated.

Rachel had returned to the garden.

—Come with me, she said.

I found myself in a situation that I could not afford to be in. It bored me to answer her questions, to have to carefully watch over my own words.

—Everything comes down to individual choice. I am a sniper of the Absolute.

But she did not accept this language. She was a practical creature. She only knew how to handle things with the secret toponymy of the night. I ceased being responsible for myself.

The Apostate came to meet us. The fungus had transformed his hands into green mushrooms. When he put them on my forehead, they smelled of must and the dampness of centuries.

—I desire the women who sit in front of me. I undress them mentally. My eyes are the passive instruments of my worst desires. They talk to me, but I don't hear them. Everything occurs inside my head, in a kind of interior darkness. I am seeking self-discipline, I drink coffee, I sit out of the sun. But nothing frees me from sin. What should I do?

I shook my head.

—I never thought you would come to this point. But let's see if we can save your soul. You have to pray.

—There is a difference: I try to tell you how difficult it is. My head hurts. My eyes. A therapy.

—I was referring to writing.

Release of the body. My double hovers somewhere between me and the inaccessible.

—The heat, he said.

He stood in shirtsleeves, took up the cup of wine in his hand and downed it in one gulp. A white light entered through the garage window. Plaster figures glowed over the closet.

—Everything is an illusion. I celebrate the inconsistency of life. I admire your willingness to make the sacrifice.

—I don't believe in anything. That gives me the strength to convince others.

—The void is not the opposite of faith, but it's necessary complement.

He was standing up, making grand gestures with his arms. In the house, I heard the immaculate voice of a woman singing. I seemed to be in a church. I went upstairs, half-opened the door leading to the living room and peeked in. I made out a white face in the dark. Red lips moved rhythmically with the music.

—I appreciate deception. It is the source of all sacrifices. There is a kind of random submission from the moment in which a project is finished.

—And death?

—It is not an obstacle. At best it will be the hypothesis of an obstacle.

There are no impossible things in this system.

He laughed.

—I hear the songs of birds and the songs of women. One of these days I'm going to climb up to the belfry and ring the bell. I want to join the legions of angels around me in broad daylight, like the fire brigade. I will order them to extinguish the fires from souls.

My headache persisted. Maybe it was my liver. With vague remorse, I put down my glass of wine and spat through the open window, trying to hit a rock. The problem was between me and Eternity.

I returned to Rachel to resolve the problem.

—I am a failure. Not: "irremediably compromised," not unrecoverable.

She tossed her head repeating the gesture to the Apostate. I felt that without my affirmation, nothing of me would survive as an example.

I am for the Revolution, though I don't know how to follow things through. During meetings, meanwhile, the most militant grow red in the face, banging on the table.

I did not manage to enter into this climate of interior torture in which all individual energies were channeled towards the suppression of an adjective or comma, or to challenge a certain attitude. Boredom made me concentrate on their faces, imagining their lives, their rooms, the books read in haste, the music listened to between political discussions. At that time, women rarely intervened; or, when they did, it was to defend the cause of the men they loved. Then, love was only an apparent sincerity leading to the identification of the body with an idea. I loved some of them silently. They had appeared to me with the diaphanous pallor of Christian virgins. They suffered and were faithful, even when their boyfriends faded into the clandestine obscurity of exile or provincial life. They knew that treason rapidly corrupts—not only the spirit, which would be secondary, but the body, which is the last stronghold in the fight against institutions. To maintain appearances, the strategic objective of these mystical creatures was to sacrifice their own pleasure.

It was an attitude that could not continue. Some eventually got married, settling in cells, stagnating hopelessly in late adolescence. Others demoted their relationships with aggression. One day, Clara called me on the telephone:

—I need to see you.

She had become associated with groups linked to the vague longing for change, embracing a survivor of one of the last revolutionary crises.

Clara remained impassive, perhaps with a more accentuated expression of irony on her face than before. She spoke in a low tone with an intense gaze. What I could see of the physical relationship between the two made me let go of all scruples.

—Do you want to go to a movie?

We agreed to meet the next day in a coffee shop downtown. I would often go to that cafe and sit alone with a closed book in front of me, limiting myself to the enjoyment of the movement of people coming in and out.

I chose a table by the door; a cold breath of air came in from outside reminding me that I was alive, distinguishable from the furniture. She arrived late.

—Are you sure you want to go?

—Your eyes resemble a baroque symphony…
I began.

She let herself become ensnared by obscure passive enjoyment. But there was something that wouldn't work.

—I am like an actor in a third-rate play. I tell you things without believing them yet feel that I am on the threshold of sincerity. If I were to take this step, I would burst into tears. But could I call this love? I can't break through the network of verbal prejudices that binds me to you.

She remained silent, playing with the lighter. Her hair covered part of her face. Her eyes moved away from mine.

—I love you! I love you!

At that precise moment I ought to have taken her hand, kissed her; instead, I stood motionless, watching the street in silence.

—It is late.

She picked up her wallet and rose to her feet. I went out after her. I didn't ask her when we would see each other again. I had begun at the end; I knew my role by heart, when in fact, it ought to have been improvised as if I was loving for the first time.

The Apostate had begun drinking again. Some rooms had already become dark. The Poet awoke.

—I was sitting in desperation in front of paper without being able to write, my hands motionless on the table.

From that moment on, he dragged out the conversation, ending up drunk. He acknowledged his failure, but what hurt him was his sterility. He knew he had left behind his best opportunities to create a work that would last. Time wearied him.

He had not managed to resist such fatigue and arrived exhausted at dusk, eyes red, as if he had suffered the most appalling insomnia.

—Yesterday I was with Clara. But it's all over.

He listened indifferently. Could he love her? Love was one of those phenomena that only superficially existed in his life. Only a foundation of self-love could stimulate him to defend the romantic relationship; not even his self-confidence counted.

—It is not likely that I will be with her again. I don't want to find her.

I left him flipping through philosophy books. It was a charade. He frequently spoke of suicide, but constantly searched out reasons to go on living.

—Where will the deterioration of the reflexes lead me? Paula was a creature of the city. She had come to me by chance:

"Can I borrow your notes?"

I recorded each of her sentences. I hoped to use them later. It didn't have to do with love. It was, rather, a sentiment that was born through my listening to her way of chanting the words, a strange music that for a few days brought tears to my eyes. Nevertheless, I remained divided. It was my relationship with other women that justified my loyalty to Clara. Memory became an obstacle to my advancing in the direction of life. The Poet reminded me:

—There came a time when I couldn't write anymore. I had, indeed, stopped writing. "What for?" (I no longer asked, "for whom?"). The desire for exile became an end point. I collapsed like rotting fruit. A horizon without papers, the end of love— the vague calling—for memory without images. The declension of names suggested a handle of farewells, the logical rigor of relations, the raging syllables of twilight.

Taking old newspapers, bottles of wine lees, remains of nets, he climbed cliffs. The sexual nature of a cork stop suffocated him. Amidst agonizing laughter, he showed me his mechanical writing fingers. A poetic motive. A summary reduction. He advanced between jets of water, treading on a nocturnal marsh of clouds; suddenly his face became a red steering wheel against the raw light of wet headlights.

—One day I asked you if you were not fed up with yourself. You answered with an obscenity. The philosophical arguments had ended. But my mission is not to save bodies—much less souls. I enjoy seeing the progressive sinking of people around me; it confirms my reasoning.

—I try to remember without becoming emotional; feeling disturbs my soul, forcing it to close like a shell. I try to imagine you now: you are sitting alone, before a white wall. You are a painting where I can project my absurd dream of being.

He stood up, opened the window and looked out at the patio. He remembered other patios from his childhood in which there were pigeons, half-open windows, and rain dripping down cast iron drain-pipes. In the obscurity came the lukewarm moisture of late sleep between dirty sheets. "So much wasted whiteness! Life itself!"

—It was after adolescence that I began to live. Up until then I had closed myself up in books, in the arti-ficial existence of coffee tables, of pages underlined in pencil. At times, I limited myself to obsessively fixing one or another face in my mind—allusive adolescents, women whose beauty struck me down like an unexpected flash of lightning in the middle of the night! During certain instants (months, but today everything is reduced to instants) I felt that strange experience of solitude between fingers, lips, a terrible shortage of words.

He was leaning up against the windowsill, the red eyes of cigarettes lit up one after another. He was thinner than when I had known him years ago. At that time, he had just come out of a deep depression. Pain had led him to take refuge in a life of pleasure in which he quickly spent the last reserves of his humanity. He had become one of those dry beings for whom life consisted of passing one's days in search of an interior purpose. Inside of him, in fact, ideas began to lose their meaning. He was distanced from reality with the calm obstinacy of somebody who has nothing more to do than prepare for his own death. As a result, he frequently repeated himself. His speech consisted of interminable evocations, the sentences appeared ready made from innumerable previous conversations, linked together in an obsessive bundle that, for me, began to make his near destruction obvious.

He also knew that if he didn't do anything, he would accelerate that end; and for this reason, he remained motionless, trying to get closer to a pure vacuity.

—Only white purifies me—not even transparency. I confuse myself with the obscurity of transparency, with the corruption of clear spaces. White, on the contrary, degrades me, contaminates me, giving me a sinister fever from which I derive metaphysical inspiration.

—For what?

—Poems! I am a poet of white, a builder of insomnia! Everything combines to free me from the endless night.

Suddenly the sky darkened and it began to rain. The water (suggesting marshes, the sea, or estuaries) was an engulfing liquid, reminiscent of the fetal state. To understand myself was to see, in the purely physical sense of the word, a body wrapped in water.

—I wrote to avoid seeing death. My "return" (for example, to the roots of language) replaced the impossibility of another physical return which, if it were possible, would make me assume death's reality. And another function of water was to prevent me from seeing, as a result of its thickness, what the invocation of death's name concealed.

—Your death?

—I returned to it in order to re-create myself, to be reborn. My vulnerability before what I wrote was the result of the affirmative inheritance that it left me.

—What does time leave us? Philosophical delirium. In the interval of life, we can conclude that individual tragedy corresponds to a discovery that the past continues to live within us.

The end of the night arrived. The fresh wind of dawn was lifting the sand, entering the house, getting into all the corners, entering through my ears, leaving my mouth and eyes parched. This dryness corresponded to the inner sensation of a plant in agony, a carbonized soul's last grasp for water.

If existence is comprised of both past and future, how am I able to say that I am? Half sleeping figures pass before my eyes in a slow haze of tepid fumes and vapors. I could hear the sound of a motor dissipating into less dense and perceptible noises, low voices, a vague whisper. My consciousness was reduced to an underground shadow, a ghost buried under the debris of an incomplete life.

I feel that violence is the only form of redemption from the moral contingency with which I am condemned, the human law that contaminates me.

—Silence! It is the absolute…

Only then did I notice that Rachel was calling us. The Poet had laid down in the back seat. I sat down beside her.

—Follow the path of the infinite. Or rather, drive towards the dizzying curve that crosses over the vast open fields to the south of memory, where the dunes are confused with the dusk, and life corrupts thought.

Sweat was running down my face but it seemed not to matter to Rachel. She was driving slowly, looking outside at the walls which, already passing the city limits, concealed abandoned houses, remnants of old farms, dead chapels. I felt that her observations of what was outside of her was a pretext allowing her to maintain control, and that the memory of the night might return any moment.

I did not try to resist, she said. Why should I? Love can become a path towards oneself, returning one to the interior of a miniscule beam of primordial sensation. Thus, concentrating on my own source, I am able to unleash a defense mechanism which, in other circumstances, I would call suicidal compulsion.

The Poet began to wake up. He remained stretched out in the back seat paying attention to our words.

—Death is a point of passage on the way to identity. I constantly pursue the contradiction, without result, but sometimes it seems my real split materializes into two. Lately, a certain dream pursues me: my body comes out of the mirror, leaving me behind.

I am left without strength, incapable of reacting to the sudden fall of my image into the abyss.

Vague beings had already begun to appear in the streets—creatures caught in the midst of sleep, rubbing their eyes in contact with light.

Now freedom was painful to me. Memories of contractions seized my muscles, forcing me to return to the beginning, to the humid and shadowy origin, to the nebulous cavity of reason.

3

—I am possessed by biographical passion! The thirst for books! Nostalgia for mornings printed between the fingers of trees and the autumnal haze in an attic inside the soul.

I order a coffee at the bar. Behind me, amidst the muffled noise of conversations and tea cups, a voice reaches me through the resonant smoke of memory. "I'd prefer not to have my life interrupted, let me be!" The employee looks at me, not the least concerned that I'm talking to his shadow. I go out to the curb. The morning begins with romantic music. I turn off the radio. Then I notice a rapid succession of gestures, the worried exterior, the scruffy face. I experience weak convulsions of lust; I am awake but the impulse to dream hurts my earthly senses. But no: I go back to the cafe, sit down at the table, open a newspaper and read over the headlines. Finally, nothing prevents my eyes from mentally re-creating her image. She returns to torment me—acidic absence, the flow of water from distant months, fragments of an intimate unity.

—Will you light me a cigarette? I'm permanently consumed with the uselessness of intuition.

Here I interject. I pay, leaving the money on the table. I toss the paper in the trash. Then I rip up two sheets of notes—metaphysical impressions on the morning sun. I walk into the street, in the direction of the river, and I think I've suddenly found a purpose, a "destiny." But what to do with her image which I'm still dragging about, the solitary weight of years of love?

—The truth is that I am sick. My head, my stomach, my heart, though not necessarily in that order. I don't finish my projects. Lost afternoons, sleepless nights, counting pulses. The sensation of fever.

Paula advised me to stop smoking cigarettes, drinking coffee, and consuming alcohol.

—To follow the path of the bourgeoisie? To sacrifice myself for survival? You know that I am a text. What others consider life, to me does not exist. I receive an influx of existential visitors. I show them how it is possible to conserve the civilization that they are slowly destroying as they become gravestones. It is not me but my eternity that is guaranteed.

—You don't see what I'm saying: you want me to get involved with you sentimentally, for us to have a normal love. I could maintain a relationship, allow you to love me, feign my emotional commitment. Destruction.

I tried to hold her. She resisted me. I insisted:

—With you it is different. From the beginning, my eyes set eagerly upon you; I can describe in detail our first dates. The obscene relationship between conventional behavior and real thinking. The attempt to keep the ritual relationship intact frightened me as a sign of madness. Perhaps I wasn't ready for the easy manner that you appeared to me in, and my reaction to this led me to unlock the mechanism of my physical hiding place. But I am changed.

—I thought I would find you in a different disposition. You came to me with the same hesitations, the same pointless torture. You do not convince me.

—At that time, when the memory of your movements and your innocent sweet voice flooded my eyes and ears, it made me sweat, and I couldn't help but look inside, losing myself in the contemplation of interior images, searching in each of them for the diversion that would allow me to escape from your domineering obsession. I achieved nothing but the emptying of my senses, my abandonment to nothingness, to emptiness, to floating about in the various circumstances that I found myself. I remember (and in these useless memories, having spent what I ought to have lived) the times when, home alone, I said your name out loud, hoping that you would appear. You put your hand on my face; you touched me…

Nothing—remained from that time. Perhaps one or another dispersed image still remained. The rest, the same emptiness that I kept turning over in my head, made me run to meet your imaginary figure. I found myself moved by small things. The greatest feelings exasperated me. I spent a whole night listening to myself express the desire to possess you.

Fear remains. Even so, I dare to speak. Among the signs of the zodiac, it was the only one free of subjection to Destiny. Not known to predict time, I assumed the qualities of abstraction, of noise itself, the tumular moan of memory.

—The tumultuous echo of the transitory blue tree, the target. October, the autumnal void of animal desire.

I see myself entombed in an attic.

—It is becoming increasingly difficult to maintain a temporal disposition. There is a kind of disease that consists of not being able to forget that it is today, and that today is a sickness accentuated by physical signs that reveal my own detachment from my body. I surround this feeling with silence.

The verb was approaching the limit of endurance. The mystery! I heard voices. It came from a dark exterior, a vibration of inert matter. I was afraid to touch it, that is, its contact forced me to retreat.

—I fear the fetus…

I half opened the letter. I saw words whose numbed muscles wrapped around me like heavy draperies depicting hunting scenes.

—…I love you. My name is…

The night she was born.

—I'm a romantic. That's because I'm not worthy of great confidence.

One does not write with impunity. Knowledge kept inside the lines, filling up pages from one side to the other, does not protect us. One reads, but what is left in the corners of time, in moments in which solitude forces us to write, is mainly debris and the remains of blood, flesh, spent hours, life sacrificed to an impetuous fight which steals the last possibility of salvation.

—I get drunk on randomness. I trample the mortifications of Destiny. Nothing is more beautiful than the unexpected noise of water in autumnal fountains. Reckless joy rushing through my lax veins.

It grows. Diffusely. It participates in the human and the vegetable. Its hands open from the bloody flesh of decomposed bodies, but alternately, a multiple being composed of diverse fragments and a more general architecture evokes a divine construction from which I am alienated by the hesitant direction of my walk.

—I rebel against the nothing that I am. And in this manner, I retain something rather than nothing.

—I find pieces of gods in the pages of dictionaries. From the bottom of my shell I throw them morsels of bread soaked in water. They fight each other over this scarce lunch.

Now it will be too late to become aware of my own deformation. A vast configuration of liquids runs above and below me, and if I feel like an animal it is only because I still crawl, vulnerable and limited, in the arteries exposed by a wounded body. The intersection of certain perspectives are like rivers whose configurations resemble the layout of antique maps. "—O God, whose destructive will I drink and am satiated with, cover my shoulders with your pus."

I spent many of my days in the Sun, looking fixedly at my shadow. It moved continuously, embarrassed by my glance. I never talked to it. I loved it in silence, with the painful consciousness that it would always be inaccessible to me.

—An obscure look into god.

—What torture will the divine silence bring me?

The consciousness of doubt opens to a silent awakening. Under the impulse of opposing desires, I affirm that my balance is based on the definition of a name, the adjacent seas, the dialectal pronunciation of the north winds. Look how unhappy you are, you that assist the downfall of dreams and addictions, upon whose cracked lips the flies have already landed. I get up, walk between you, feed on your excrement.

—The subsequent storms, modifying the design and outline of the cliffs, opened to the broad perspective of a terrestrial curve towards the other side of the universe.

Soon after, in discussion:

—Everything is related. Not in an obvious way, but in obscurity, as if by design.

I recognize myself in these words and approach, or rather, my shadow pursues a body endowed with the wisdom of ancient prophets. I draw nearer to the great mysteries and breathe in the scent of winter waters.

—The movements of a flower parallel those of a penis in its illuminated awakening.

—Women, the wet leaves of the large Nordic trees.

They give me something to eat. Paranoia is a scared dog during a storm of sunflowers. All previous generations have died. Bent over by doubt, I accept the gods. Nostalgia is the desire not to be me. Dissolution is insipid. I drink the monotony of light, without scepters, without nimbuses, without halos.

—I transformed normal behavior into a caricature and the fall into an exaltation.

All interrogations are accidental and peripheral

It was one of those nights. Gnawed by boredom, I considered breaking out—a cold country, a uniform landscape, poetic cities. The air vibrates, damp from the recent rain and wind in the night.

—The birds were retiring to the wharfs along the coastline. The ships remained far off. During such times, when I heard music, I often thought of leaving. I formulated omens, which I brought forth as desperate evidence—of my renunciation and non-resistance. I took advantage of the unparalleled expectation of the decision. Neither truth nor obscurity—a game, figures, places. Excess itself.

I smoke calcium in splendor. I reach the Orient. Pain is the fugitive joy of creation. There are maritime steps in the eyes of maritime drunkards. The Guardian of Hymen is ossified in the interior augur of the instant. I am amazed to find myself almost Indian.

Paula had left me alone at the corner next to the cafe. The afternoon sun stunned me. In the bright obscurity I could just distinguish a figure approaching. It was the Apostate.

—No, I'm sorry. I don't have time to listen to you, but if you've come here to say that next week someone will be waiting for me with a scythe in his hand, then I am ready. All lives are of limited duration, like contracts, and the world, of which I am momentarily a part, imposes temporary obligations. I have a certain reluctance to impose my views yet realize that they are the ones which end up imposing themselves. In the reality of this dark cavity, they have no alternative.

Here, leaned up against the wall, having gotten used to his presence, I interrupted his speech. He laughed, sat down, drank some water and started to speak again. It was then that I noticed that he looked like a beardless Christ with a golden halo around his eyes. His bones appeared transparent, especially in his hands, and between his body and the wall there formed a cloud of great luminous intensity, where his glance was insensibly directed. Perhaps he had tried to transform himself, but I didn't notice it. What is certain is that when an angel, or a blackbird, came through the window, neither one of us felt able to think. Something was influencing my sensitivity. I inhabited a spherical form, similar to a uterus, from within which I answered questions put to me. My responses illuminated the arrangement of the space like a flashlight with worn out batteries.

—The motive of prophecy, someone had told me, involves the study of suggestion. No oracle can contradict the Future, since oracles contain the future's very possibility.

From a distance the most common things appear even more evident to the extent that all the virtual qualities of uniqueness (and simplicity) come in contact with them, touch them and are interfused by them. There are abilities therefore, not only of foreseeing the distant future, but also of discerning intimate speech, of which I adhere to the tone, and according to which I propose to change my own body. I shall be told that silence always brings up new conceptions in the context of primitive memory. It is better that the return is consumed, so that life itself can stultify in permanent desire for another life. Afterwards, I never forgot how monstrous harps of virile fingers swelled, vanishing into dust and blood. Such a sterile wish, such a weak will... Suddenly, rotten provisions, smelling of discontentment, fall from my satiated mouth. Before my lips had tried them (and even then, or when I received them in communion, I knew concretely what death felt like in the throat and wrists). Suddenly full of amorous inclinations, I opened and closed my arms over nothing, and from the fatigue of many years, exclaimed:

—The powerful light is dead, and yet there remains an excess of passion.

On the other hand, they had already heard me. I crossed through the flowing wall without banging my head on the plaster, and I noticed a body propped up at the table with a brain in his hands. Apparently, he slept. Earlier, while sitting there, I knew that he was dreaming, and I had no other intention than to reconstitute his unique being.

—Believe me!

And to keep it that way, evoking the blackened face of the primitive inhabitant, I myself replaced him, returning to the house of worship. I entered the rooms and bedrooms, and went out to the balconies. And when I reached the height of the ceiling my feet were bleeding.

4

A little earlier, immobility had seemed infinite. The paradox perpetuated in my head; ideas I had formulated broke through the cocoon of my spirit, launching themselves against all logical reasoning. A combination of arguments resolved the initially perceived confusion, the least audible connection crumbled, waking me from an almost mathematical ecstasy. A dream about numbers prevented me from forming an image. In the distance one could hear music: a regular progression of sounds and singing, mixed with the coastal noise of trees and birds brought by the wind.

The whole situation was definitive. What was standing over me and around me had settled into a static model, initiating a rotating movement that found its exact axis in me. My shadow, projected into the hollow center of a human life, appeared in the interstices of the landscape, acquiring the essence of gesture and formula. What I thought to be my own authentic being was dissipating in the neutral zone between my body and the ground; meanwhile, I looked to the sun for protection from this kind of vacuum; and the sensation of heat resulting from physical contact with light gave me an impression of life which, at each instant, seemed threatened by shadow. I was able to remain lucid while the darkness had not yet corroded the clarity of my features.

I entered into the cavity of the dream. Clouds tore my skin with their metal edges, and small birds drank the blood that gushed from my wounds. I was seated on a human torso and everything was burning all around me. I cannot precisely put together the circumstances of the transformation; only the sudden passage from day to night gave me the notion that all I had known was definitively dead.

—I understand the struggle between the conflicting limitations of human and animal.

Realizing that they did not want any explanation from me, I grew silent.

After the rupture, the contradiction that I had long foreseen between myself and the group was finally dissolved. The end of love, even if it was only a relatively normal fact in the course of events, had disturbed me to the point of having made me stop looking for the crack which I had begun to foresee.

—The pathway branched out from a certain point: to the wooded alleys protected from the sun and people's glances, to the unpaved path. I opted for the latter. It took me down to the sea. This idea appeared to me like something musical, a resonant path that would blend me with the birds and the sound of the wind in the shrubs: an escape from temporal progression."

Instead, I suddenly bend over the side of the carriage to vomit. The wind hits me on the head with intensity, and my vision is constrained by the light.

The green treetops, the morning sky. Melancholy. Grey. Being is revealed in its pact with the very life that animates one's hands: a light that comes from within. Agitation fills the windows. The sudden fall of leaves coincides with the destiny that I put to my step. Printed between the chain and the face, the text, seen through transparently, resembles a body. The arid voice communicates in its original construction. Multiple lips at the beginning of a sentence: sonorous cupolas, echoes, arms shattered in an explosion of insomnia. The fragment reborn from the total appearance of the night—is carried by a messenger of black contours towards the blue horizon. Then everything tumbles. But I only remember immobile things.

We had arranged the meeting by phone. She laughed as usual, spoke of disagreements, of a failed love. I didn't realize the meaning of her words. I expressed myself without clarity. I couldn't explain what I truly felt; my ideas were scattered. She had a way of pretending that she heard what I was saying: love was only a symptom of a more general code that made us never reveal the inner reality of our existence.

—As long as I'd loved her, poetic expression coincided with my most "humane" self. Sincerity and "humanity" infiltrated my verses, and each stanza stained the page as an authentic feeling, making me suffer. But poetry has no body; its missing fingers hurt me in every line I wrote, and my situation brought me closer to disease and madness. Reading to myself out loud, I called her. A magical process, a ritual, a way to evade solitude, to forget the useless reality of her detachment. For this I sacrificed my own "life" to achieve a closeness to others, escaping myself, to arrive at a common presence. I'd lived with her image; it arose from the whiteness of the page, her face smiles at me as usual, and a background of trees projects the illusive reality of her virtual existence, reduced to words, sound games, the hopeless obscurity of the metaphor.

I spoke now with my shadow. The flowing waves were covering it. I stood breathless, drowned in thought until fatigue made me move. Much later I discovered that beyond exhaustion, a defense mechanism had arisen against the current of my memory, drawing out of me what it had formed in my spirit.

I made a truce with sleep. When I awoke, the sun had already set. The cold wind made me lucid. Perhaps I had reached the objective which had long been traced out: the eventuality of death was closing in. Again, the images that I had sketched out before falling asleep returned, and the absence of Clara tormented me.

—The decision to love penetrates me like a dagger. The last light of the soul fades. I sing a final breath of restlessness.

Paula sat down beside me.

—Possibly you won't realize the change, nor will you divert your thought from the line at the end of the page. But when I speak, your look modifies each of my words. It is not through the casual influence of physical attraction that your presence is permitted. Time diverts the hands of the one who writes under the table, where they huddle around the fire rising from the earth's interior. You talk of long ago. It is certain that I cannot draw any coincidence from this sudden encounter with a voice and an image as if both belonged to the same human and abstract body. The regular process of the transformation of thoughts, the passage from ancient forms of imagination to a state closer to "nothing", occasionally impacted my "I"; the result was that I could only survive with the intention to do so. The journey of the line provides me with this possibility: I experiment with the return. The desolation of meaning, the desolation of the senses, are the necessary faces I inscribe in the final unity. I age them or save them in my stagnant memory. I tell you that my eyes are burning. Two balls of fire. Oh, if my soul only knew how to penetrate you. A breath pulls me, I spin inside of it confounding my words, entangled in the labyrinth of your ears. I will do it. Do I burn inside you like posthumous fire? Her mouth had the confusing syntax of cherries.

—I did not see Clara again. I limited myself to imagining her, always from a distance. One day, she crossed the street in the direction of a free standing house. It was a grey afternoon. Another time, I bumped into her in the hallway of a building. Her hair was the only thing I noticed.

I reached the limit and turned back. Patiently I followed my own footsteps, hesitating to take a new path. I did not recognize myself in those steps and was trying to reconstitute, through the path taken in reverse, the mental mechanism that had initiated the separation.

—Like migratory birds. But to where?

—It is simple. It involves searching for relationships between objects with the intention to develop a complex systematization of their self-perceptions.

—Something similar happens in real life. As it advances we begin to distinguish what is going on behind the trees and bushes. Strange constructions destroyed by vegetation, dried bodies of small animals, illegible inscriptions—a landscape of ruins which, despite everything, retains a deep inner logic.

I peeked out the window and saw the sea. A cloud covered the sun and it started to rain along the shoreline.

—We began our ascent.

—Our actions have cosmic utility. Somewhere, this is being registered, and when it is suitable, someone will remember to reveal it to someone else.

The Poet gave me a handwritten sheet of paper.

—My objective was to experiment with my own death: I began by recovering an unusable text fragment. A travel narrative was deployed. I gave it a name, and it materialized into a human figure, endowed with the ubiquitous double quality of body and text. The body died, but the text remains alive and talking.

I didn't feel satisfied.

—It is very simple. A disposition for the Infinite requires more than an intention.

Arriving at this point, it was useless to try to return. What was in store for me could be death, but if it was something else, the result would be the same. And when I kissed Paula, I found that there was no difference between me and the Apostate. I laughed.

—After all, what you want is to talk with yourself, said the Poet.

—It is true, but the truth is also not the truth: maybe I won't look at myself in the mirror any more; perhaps I will not find another mirror; meanwhile, perhaps the winter will arrive, and I will depart.

—I choose the latter hypothesis.

—I still don't understand, said Paula.

—Now it's all too simple.

END OF SEPTEMBER
(AT NIGHT IN A HOTEL ROOM)

"I'd complained of excessive light. I put my hands over my eyes, obscuring the world—and life itself. I proclaimed myself an atheist. Yet I felt that some divine essence manifested itself in words. "Poetry"—a gift, he said. It was enough to feel a superiority that others censured me for; and for this, friends were scarce. "Exile is my obligation," someone wrote in a letter.

—I have orientation problems. The north, the south, the very notions of space and perspective baffle me. Errors, the failed gaze, a vague sense of lost friendships due to a shortage of gestures.

Perhaps I gave too much to myself. Meanwhile, I went about without knowing who I was. Writing intermittently about my life, filling notebooks with an obscure hard to decipher penmanship…I wanted to leave nothing to others. I discovered that I didn't like myself; and that's why I couldn't—or didn't want to—advance towards a self-love that was strange to me.

As a result, I became sick. It was winter. Emaciated, I walked through the streets at night far from the center, aiming my curses at lampposts; this image still remains. I did not arrive through my words. I let them follow a stream, from which self-regeneration became possible. I had a strange lust to consume myself, to destroy the remains of a past in which, possibly, I had known instants of fullness.

I no longer wondered who could help me. Whenever there occurred the chance to rekindle a relationship, or to find a face that remained in my memory, I wasted it! Tears bothered me. I was given to morbid sentimentalism, a compassion for myself, which gave me pleasure: the satisfaction of intimate torture. I'm not able to reread what I write. My old texts pile up, without order, without an interior nexus, accumulating their own contradictions. In the instant in which I grasp them, my whole life is revealed to me—completely useless. At last, my connectedness to my own dreams and transformations are lost. I stagnate, and thus I rot.

—I returned to poetry as an exorcism. No! Poetry is nothing. I cannot attribute to myself the illusion of a movement of repetitions and setbacks, of imprecise anxieties, of the amorphous shape of larva.

Yesterday I took her hand. She became indifferent, limp. I passed the day without understanding her attitude. I left her at the door to the cinema without saying goodbye. Will I return to see her again? Something about her nature eluded me. Everything always seemed to be without a tomorrow. It was for this that I loved her. As regards to the rest—her hands, her face, her breasts, her sex—the physical elements of a relationship—it was a misconception that I had become a victim.

I am afraid of getting sick. The madness would remove me definitively from what she left me—the memory of her absence. How to find her again, to distinguish her from her shadow?

The day was white, without rain, without cold. I sweated. I didn't check my temperature. But my arms and joints hurt. I rot.

I am approaching a phase of corruption. I voluptuously give myself to renunciation—and renounce my own being. I no longer wonder about myself, nor about the interrupting consequences which at times leave my interlocutor suspended, producing suspicion, irony—and, always, distance.

I lose my last friends. I become inaccessible. I create an ambiguous personality and get lost in my labyrinth. I limit myself to watching birds, looking for meaning in their migration. I see them disappear and afterwards return, and I try in this obscure movement to encounter a part of my soul.

—In my head, reason is the eye of a dead fish. I throw it against the wall, trying to crush it. My face is filled with pus, fear, indecision. Where to direct my footsteps? How can I find her—and her abstract hands, the obscure line of her lips—now that I have lost myself?

Not even death will save me. But I begin to prepare for it, abandoning my impulse to be with others, for contact, and sensation. I touched her, and she pulled away, leaving me empty, without any chance for deliverance.

Then I return to life. Or rather, to the chagrin of being, to the interior crisis that left me exhausted:

two nights of insomnia, loneliness, talking to myself, lying on the floor, pawing myself in the old woods.

—How to define myself? I lost myself in this fragment of the past in which her absence was manifested. Without explanation. In the instant that the gods turned against me.

But could it have been any other way? I ask. What was the purpose of allowing myself to be persecuted without a goal? To try to retrace her journeys, gestures, encounters? I limited myself to following her shadow. She was already lost forever in a remote corner of my life.

I began to get frightened when I noticed that I wasn't able to write her name. I picked up a sheet of paper, and when I began to write a letter—a place, a date—an unexplainable force prevented me from continuing. Covered in tears, I read the letter on the white paper out loud, ripping it up afterwards.

I didn't write to her again. I felt her next to me. I held her body with the conviction of a bad actor. I abandoned everything to experience the insatiable momentary relationship, the superficiality of repeated dialogues.

—I know that she exists, but not for me. I exist in the place where she left her trace, an echo of phrases that I'm incessantly forgetting.

One time I tried to see her. But it wasn't her; it was what she had left behind of herself in my life, and that sustained the torment of a presence that dominates me, inhibiting my being, keeping me suspended in an impossible gesture.

Who, at last, would betray the pact of love that united us? Or would this love, already independent of the casual relationship between two people, remorselessly continue to pursue me? How long could I continue this fidelity to a phantom, this terror of losing, along with her memory, my ultimate justification for being?

—I no longer had somebody I could turn to. Until then, I had functioned as my own absolute confidant who, at the same time, betrayed the trust that had been put in me—with the revelation in the texts that I continued to write of my journey of falling. By preventing myself from reading what I had written, I finally destroyed that interior relationship that was vital to me. Sleep already occupied a substantial part of my thoughts which moved along with the subterranean logic of dreams, and I lived in an exterior vertigo that consumed me in artificial plenitude.

I began to drink again. It was a way to restore my humanity. Re-entering a relationship with myself was a process. At dawn, after I threw up, I lay down on the bench in front of the house feeling the cold numbing of my body as lucidity approached. "The cold was my only link with the real."

The Poet had fallen asleep. He was there in the iron bed between religious images and empty medicine bottles. His face maintained the expression that I had seen on him shortly before when he had confessed to me. With his hands hidden in the pockets of his old worn winter coat, I noticed his long fingers and thick nails, the way he put his hands on the tabletop, the movement of his arms while he was speaking. He awoke from the torpor in which the first moments of contact with another reality had plunged him; he spoke as if just then discovering his words, and yet an interior reflection of wisdom guided his speech. Crystal tears separated the divide between dusk and dawn in the premature aging of his eyes; and he did not weigh the necessity of taking refuge in himself, or perhaps he no longer suspected himself. He was attracted beyond measure by others, by his contact with them, by the search for a transient relationship. Lost in continuity or in the prospect of succession; and without taking initiatives (as he appeared towards the end! A vague cupula of life! An undecided suspension of voice!) he approached us without implying what had already ravished his hallucinatory fires of melancholy.

Something in him was exposed: a voluntary effort to remain sacrificed for what was limited to gesture, to authentic mortal exhibition. I'm not talking about the rough sketch of the sentence, which I think is excessively spontaneous: "life did not make an effort in him," etc. Only what truly happened would persist. The sound of bells had woken him from an obscure dream featuring symbols of the ultimate opacity of the underground world. Like one who gives in, he hurries up; his gaze accompanies his dreams of words; anxiety succeeds sorrow, and it touches him at that precise moment in his life when he has become common, vulnerable to the proof of the end. Where I've felt weak is in the obstinacy of her name—rather than in the hope that she would return. But where he is, things are authentic, the thick noise of the old wood flows from the walls, from the roofs, from the frames, from hollow headboards. The book that has been closed for years still remains under his tarnished gaze. The flies are buzzing around his grey lips, his hair still shines (it was a day at the end of autumn) under the warm sun, his waist cuts the perpendicular horizon. His bare feet create roots in the earth.

—Now it is all too simple, I repeat.

Clara's absence had ceased to amaze me. I had loved her in a time of innocence and what remained of this love, in my memory, was still wrapped in light. Sometimes, lightning illuminates certain moments of my life which I had thought to be unquestionably forgotten, and my face fills with tears. My lips formulate a concept:

—Truth escapes me; my mind conceals it.

Paula repeated the phrase several times, laughing. My expression came close to lunacy. Would Clara deserve it? I imagined her close to me. I touched her, predicting her answers, and despite not externalizing my emotions, I ended up surprising myself by the unexpected changes in the environment. I looked around and recoiled, frightened, as if something pursued me.

—Is she dead? Between who I was and what I am going to be, the days do not count.

—The real problem is afterwards.

—Not the real problem, but the closest thing to a sort of fair assessment of reality.

I had no answer, not because I couldn't give one, but because a positive or negative definition of an answer had not occurred to me. I was searching for its exact meaning—and meanwhile, persistently avoiding a positive attitude. Thus, I kept myself at the edge of doubt, just for the pleasure of feeling it circulating inside of me.

—The technique may be accurate, but it is not everything.

—Try to understand me, the Poet said theatrically.

—I left out telling you what, in my conversation with Clara, was essential: the definition of love. Many times, I have told you that I loved her, but the way I told you did not translate the complexity of the feeling that connected us. Love is a relationship too fragile to define what existed between us. Perhaps a connection for life, one being in the absence of another. She was part of me, and yet I felt her to be entirely detached from me, as if she were outside the bundle of my feelings and emotions. Was this excessive? I couldn't help feeling this way, though I hadn't sufficient clarity to say this to her.

Only now the evidence appeared to me, an accusation of my own spirit that had allowed itself to remain tied to the elusive love of a shadow of itself, to the point of dissipation, leaving me immersed in nothing: an abysmal absence where I was the unique center.

—The separation, which ultimately defined me, would be the singular process to solve my interior problem. Now that my soul is a huge empty hole, I will surrender to it without ceasing to search for it, despite never finding anything.

5

During the last lucid days of autumn
Diana's statue by the entrance of the park
There, between trees, green, the undulation
of the lake leaves Fall suddenly Lingering in the air
then land upon the damp Night earth
the ultimate declension—Paula enters the cafe. She
doesn't see me right away. I look at her against the
white light of the station square, vaguely thinking:
love, one of the unexpected things with which my
soul has been confronted, but always without assum-
ing the appropriate attitude, a haste about reaching
absurd objectives, the apparent indifference, the
immobility, the low sky. We cross the street. Everything stops when I hold her hand, my first contact
with her skin. She hesitates. I complete the ritual.
We kiss. The bus returns to its route. The passengers
stare at me intently. I see their teeth filling up their
faces, yellow and large, transforming into dark finely
wrought mahogany furniture, hollow trunks. The
elevator closes between us. When the door reopens

I encounter the doorman. I feel like I am being watched. I stick my pen in his wild boar nose and it starts bleeding. I run up the stairs to the terrace. I enter an abandoned garden. The herbs had invaded the flowerbeds, penetrating their walls and leaving a humid rotting mass in view. I gather the fingers of plaster statues, filling my pockets. I begin to raise the sheaves towards the top. A glazed dome hides me from the sky; grey light dazzles me. I fall into the well of an elevator. I'm lying on the bottom, dirty with oil. I vomit a dark paste. The plaster fingers are moving around in my pocket, they grab my prick, I begin to run. A wild boar chases me. I fall into Clara's lap. It is a wet meadow and the rain licks my wounds. Her familiar face leans against mine. She kisses me. I push her away, with my head still full of images.

—What was that?

—I'll explain everything.

I asked for another cup of coffee. But I did not confess that I had decided once again to pursue Clara. My need to see her superimposed itself on the very death of the past. It had begun to rain. People took shelter under the awning at the entrance. A multitude of people invaded the cafe talking loudly. I put money on the table and walked towards the pier. The wind bent the trees, the smell of wet earth pervaded the air. A sequence of thoughts about Clara returned to my mind. I was contriving a way of seeing her again without her being aware of my presence. I would anxiously pursue her around town; without her it would not be possible to survive.

When I sat down again at the table in the cafe I was soaking wet.

—The rotten remains of a generation piled up in my mouth. The more I vomit the more it sprouts from the firmament of my soul. I spit out decomposed fragments in torrents, the remains of sex...

A decision was gradually forming inside me. Paula's silence persisted. I kept myself still, my objective now was to resist the transitory identification of movement and death.

It continued to rain. Seagulls landed on the half-buried hull stretched out on the beach between old broken amphorae. The grey sky had a morbid look. My presence in the cafe appeared real when in fact I was at the beach.

—Was it me?

I looked at the strange figure that asked me this question. I seemed to see myself in the mirror; the voice I heard was my own voice. And it was I who started to run after the birds, injuring myself on the edges of the hull. I ended up stretched out on the sand. Nothing would change my conviction that it was I, nor would a blue mediocrity on the horizon dissipate the leaden atmosphere. The wind picked up, pushing away the lower clouds. Words in swarms come together on my lips so abstractly that not even their memory is preserved in my fingers. Hesitantly, I searched the roof of my mouth. One afternoon, the horizon before me reminded me of how I had tried to represent the useless comedy of love. Would Paula have believed me? I only now started talking to myself about "truth". And how about the past? In that instant, questions followed each other from the apparent repose of "being". I touched the sand, feeling its hardness, but there did not appear to me to be an end to the necessary credibility (a quality that separates the imaginary from reality).

—Donatello? Italy. White spring.

Masts. Masters. Noise of horses (minstrels on the way). Harps tear Beatrice's dress. In the sick mouth, the lips split the sentence: I love/you. Beauty. Seagulls take refuge in poetry. Prosaic insects dive into the water in anchored flight. The heart welcomes the rising star. It survives another night of vague nightmares. The carriage in the sea.

Let's meet in the arch. The air brings us the hollow word. The hand tills the humid lap. The dark night protects the lovers. I fall through a crack in the boat. The deep bottom. Before you—the full world. The body pours out over the deck. New ways of expression dominate sentence construction. Emotion. It searches for the shape of the hand not reducible to the shell receptacle of the lamp. Your dull eyes. Sparkles of silver. More wine in port drawers, water in the shadow. The dawn sick with old discolored photographs breaks the mechanical image. Hope of final agonies.

Something stirs under the tree. Twilight, decadence. The lip itself emphasizes the modification of the initial tone. Let time erase it.

—Pay attention to page limits. The folded sheet forming a triangle.

I began to get used to relatively short dialogues from which I composed short autobiographical sequences. Later I would reduce them to memories. The future foretold only a few certainties: the use of language for systematic destruction and the worship of an absence without object.

—The sentence does not accurately designate the entire clause. Dementia consists in the subjection to rigid rules of separation. I believe in excessive rigor.

One glance cuts out pieces of landscape. Not at random. An exhalation from the past lays its breath upon me, and I transform myself into the shape of fossilized rocks. Color is fundamental in the choice of elements. Solar division of nature. The gaze only defines traces of sentences interrupted by words like holes. Rocks, trees: white space in the abstract crossing of ideas. To examine, to rewrite: the ears that suddenly get scared. The thickness of the page. Dead fingers waiting for resurrection.

—Love. Tragedy of duration.

There was something breathless, an orthographic repugnance. Still at the cafe, while it was raining,

I observed Paula. One day I had given her a bracelet with the inscription "I LOVE YOU" engraved in red. She laughed.

—To make what is impermanent endure. The journey continued in sparsely furnished rooms. I hid out of spiritual necessity. I needed to feel far away from myself.

Clara called me. We got together. The places and gestures were always the same. Afterwards, I noticed that the fault was in ourselves. Desire aroused this fount of destruction.

The Poet listened. He was affected by the disgrace of existence. He resigned himself to solitude, and not even when he was forced to act would he abandon his voluntary sadness.

—Sacrifice is a stigma of the soul. It is also the best proof that it exists.

And that was enough to justify himself. In this way he redeemed his days spent in bed, the late nights at the window, observing the changing of the seasons by the sparseness of the trees along the sidewalk.

I balanced myself in front of the window, my face against the glass. Paula reached out her hand in the hallway. "In this shadow we will survive everything. Even the death of the gods." She stood standing, leaning against the compartment door. A little earlier, she had given me the impression that she was about to fall; now, the words sustained her, they made her solid.

The scenario changes. Here is the beach, the sea, the end of an autumn afternoon. I say her name and she approaches. Her fingers hurt like the branches of a mad poplar. Bells ring obstinately in my head while I kiss her eyes. Luminous spheres. My burning lips spit out the remains of pupils. The fishermen are approaching, they gather around me. We enter the tavern. I see them laughing with their red teeth shining at dusk, large distant clouds rush onto the horizon. My voice recites nonsensical verses. I am alone. I left her in the middle of the night, expecting that the waves would cover her and drag her up against the rocks.

When she returned, shattered by fish and the underwater currents, she was smiling. "You didn't wake me up. I arrived without a childhood. I follow the paths of the image. I lost myself on shore…" And she pushed me down to the bottom. "Now the hands touch the edge of the window," she said. She continued: "I established a point situated between a dream and what I thought to be reality." When I left her she was very quiet, only her lips trembled. But inside, her tears were crushed like moist petals of morning dew. That lifeless face, the silence of the house, the obsessive memories, left my mouth dry. I couldn't tell her anything, neither of the body hidden under the flowers, nor of the white hands.

In the street, as I walked away, I wondered if my peace was not similar to a rainfall of sick angels.

There are days when the image of the past paralyzes my movements. For the chance of conviction, I give myself up to spiritual wanderings. I lean backwards in successive movements until I crash my head against the wall, then forwards, until I lean over the well. My face is reflected blindly in the bottom, and in the place of my nose there's a red hole, obscene and obscure, where huge silent fish swim in heat. I pull the rope, return to the dream, cross the street, and enter the garden. I suffer from vertigo between columns of ivy and injure myself in the shrubs, avoiding the stone benches whose sinuous shadows divide lovers. The arm of a violin brushes against me, crinkling my skin, and music gushes out of my ears along with the capsule of a dented bullet, the remains of a nasal bone, and brain fragments. I collect my last thoughts, scattered in gravel; one of the eyes still turns luminous and blue on the horizon. The other one—the tadpole in the pond, hastened the metamorphosis. Ah yes, further behind: the house, the curve in the road, the waxed furniture, the wooden floor. The window open to air out the musty smell. The green earth. Cold days, dispersing elements, I. It brightens up. Music of birds, bloody wings, silex of fires upon the crest of minutes. The howl of the madman cuts the sonorous navel of the mother. "It doesn't rain, mother, it doesn't rain in the black light of acids and saps, it doesn't rain in the corollas of the city of Upsilon, nor in the petrified tree branches or in the fingers falling like hail!" On calm days you could hear the rope shrinking around the hangman's neck. I abolish the distance between dreams and the life of roots corrupted by fish. I begin to laugh in a flow of electric sensations, spitting out pieces of myself. I climb up to the green, along the fierce edge of the soul. I am in the eternal day, hearing the voice of my spirit wearing the tattoos of sailors. I rise above the clouds and they move away, revealing decomposing leaves, cigarettes, purple flashes of the absolute, the pier—smooth columns.

—And how about these sail boats?

It seemed like time suspended its course. Her lips moved speaking confusing phrases that my ears sometimes mistook for the noise of the wind or the music of the harp in the deserted hall. I follow her through a strange tangle of corridors and doors. Owing to their transparency, her feet don't touch the ground. I can see her body clearly in the luminous fluctuations of the water, liquid nakedness. On the landing, she disappears without turning back; when I call out to her, my voice sounds entirely strange to me.

—Perhaps everything had been imaginary; but how could I believe myself, if the cold impression of her skin remains intact on the lips that I kiss her with? Or if her last look, anxious and ecstatic, pulls me into a hell of love without hope?

The tepid tedium of travel, endless landscapes, images of houses. Before arriving at the demolished wall of the station under the volcanic cylinder of water, there are iron stairs. The wind sweeps my hair into my eyes. I walk towards the beach. I hear screams from afar. I wave. It is a normal gesture. A sudden gift to the anonymous. The delivery of one body to another, both staring attentively at the already closed food stands, the abandoned watchtowers, the cry disappearing on the horizon against the echo of the mountains. We enter the woods; a warm breath numbs me under the pines. We used to kiss in front of the manor house. It was abandoned, sheltering wooden chests, forgotten attics, dust, furniture gnawed by woodworms, and old lamps. We would discuss politics, literature, listen to the news, present utopian solutions in the face of our fragile, hurried calendar-led lives, while memories brought us to other places, to the first few days of autumn with the leaves sticking to our feet, wet from the sludge, the task of putting them in buckets, sweeping the stone, slowly, picking up the leaves one by one, examining the veins, yellowing, the breaking point, tree branches crossed at their heights, the sun, the lack of wind, my hand touching your sex for the last time before our return to the city.

There, Clara still had a body. The opening was indistinguishable from the source of life, from where it began to sprout green branches of spring and moss. The tepid warmth of shadows along the walls. With half-closed eyes, I saw tiny flickering particles in the atmosphere whose feathers covered my body like an obscure disguise, which I called souls. An infinite breath buzzed around me in the physical form of a bee, which Clara drove away with her hand. I held it, making sure that the wound would lead to her dispersion into an abstract circle of pure essence. She laughed and fled to the sun, transfigured by an abrupt appearance of light into the figure of love, which in the following moment, by an almost imperceptible sway of the tree tops, restored me to her carnal and elusive presence. I knew then that I would not see her again.

When I came to myself, the train was pulling out. The image of Clara had dissipated completely, and it was in vain that I searched my pockets for an old photograph that she had given me. Sheets of hastily written notes, bus tickets, lunch vouchers, interrupted poems, obscenities.

—What is that, asked Paula.

I read:

—Your eyes are flesh and blood, and I am inside of them. I am there without being inside myself.

She could not hear me. The station began to fall behind me. Everything looked familiar: the compartment, the people. If I were to stand up, my movement would impact each side of my body in physical symmetry with the others on the train. An apparent relationship would take place between me and them.

—If I was at the window, if I knew that Clara was looking at me, that this precarious balance would not be destroyed…

I returned to the beginning with the progressive reduction of the sentence. I opened the window to let the cold air enter so that the twilight would agitate our bodies and souls.

—I travel aimlessly within myself. That is, I continue in the direction of a point that I cannot define. Maybe it's death. It has the face of Clara. I need to concentrate on another idea.

I felt the fresh wind and soot from the machine. I closed the window again. In front of me Paula was reading. The world was beginning to make sense.

—Something unites us along the way to where I am going. The twilight will release its grey wings over my former body. Images float around me.

One could already see the ocean.

—Clara!

Her hair covered part of her forehead and fell over her shoulders. Paula looked at me. Incomprehension was taking form. The noise of the rails increased the malaise, eating parts of her sentences. Marking the page with her index finger, she put down the book.

—The Poet assured me that the answer was waiting for me at the end of this line. Where is the end? A while ago I thought you were waiting for me. I was really convinced that I would find you. But now I know that I came here for nothing.

Solitude recommenced my inquietude. This wisdom came to me:

—Death is one of the functions of the soul.

I had arrived early to the middle of my life. If I wanted to die, in fact, the twilight would resemble a blood-stained sheet. I could hear the sound of the wind in the crevices of the carriage, in the cracks of my ears. I saw the Poet weakening, losing his breath. I held his skull in my hands, asphyxiated by doubt. I put my coat over him, but he remained cold. I stayed sitting, gazing at Paula, inventing a possible love scenario that I had not previously imagined.

—Everything that depends on something detaches itself from the plum line.

The noise of the train resembled a typewriter. My ideas began to modify into a line tangential to my own intentions. From a random feeling I passed on to an awareness of the process of creating diverse emotions, but it followed by accident.

—What do you have?

I noticed now that Paula was staring at me.

—Excerpts of Eros. Reunion of fragments. What our epoch feels is the intelligence of desire. All the rules are to be formulated.

I couldn't continue. I had drunk several cups of coffee, but the fever had shaken my lucidity. The sickness cheated me at each instant.

—Posterity doesn't favor concise beings.

My face was in absolute denial of what I said. I lacked a physiognomy that could distinguish me from myself.

—It is I!

And I lay down on a bench exposing a wound in my arm vanishing into pus.

—How to survive one's own decomposition? How to survive?

I had already left my anxiety behind. I focused on something vaster and more imprecise, at the dark dawn where humanity begins.

—Somewhere, on the other side of the earth, lies an unexplored frozen island whose inhabitants feed on our souls and who are the grotesque echo of our own lives. They worship the Absolute. It is a spongy and volatile kind of being. They've built a mechanism based on complicated magnetic qualities to maintain themselves. People become serious when they are close to it, remaining in silence for hours; on their faces one can see the furrows left by heavy tears. The next thing you know we're trapped in a machine floating on a higher sphere of reasoning. A strong suggestion of divinity.

She let me talk. I discovered little by little the emergence of a dizzying grammar whose nature I had not yet foreseen.

—I began to concentrate on a metal fragment ripped from the heart of a subterranean bird with the inscription: *The fundamentals of being are to be found in the shelters of time.* Something was bringing me back to myself. I was suspended in a frame. I thought I was the only one who could find the key.

—The beginning is in each point of the walk, said the Poet.

This made no sense. I repeated:

—The beginning...

An emptiness in thought had opened from within me. I repeated the sentence again until it made me moan. The scarce light of dawn revealed the approaching end of the trip.

—I came looking for myself.

—It is I.

We were both, but we both were our own contradiction. Everything was in doubt.

—It is I. I am the vast spaces. I am the vertigo. I am the passing of time over the crags and coastal cliffs. It would have been I if it was not me, and yet it is also I.

—Something excludes itself, I conclude.

The question, however, emerged on the horizon in the place of the sun.

Relinquishing my old convictions, I entertained myself by composing aphorisms: losing your virginity is less important than losing your life; and this other one: lose time making a living.

The repetition of this "aphorism" induced me to imagine a breviary on banal thought, including the banal method itself. Without philosophical depth, yet striving for it as an ultimate objective, this breviary would consist of several literary "genres": poetry, prose, theater, etc., without excluding the "generic" overcoming of the starting point.

A refined mechanism would put the principle organization into motion, and in turn, each one of its arms would put into motion small pinwheels of principles. The whole would move into the sphere, or into the idea of the sphere (and also into the sphere of the idea).

—The power to excite destiny was restored in me. Deluding myself momentarily, I closed my eyes so that, in the artificially created darkness or obscurity, clear "abstract" vision would arise. I do not believe that the "original presence" of Number has been verified. In its place is a confused notion of a god who gathers together the initially suggested fragments. Consequently, when necessary, a secondary intervention reproduces the original image under a blurred poetic form.

—And so it happened, that being alone on the beach, I decided to react against disappointment and boredom. I went to the mouth of the river. There I stood, watching the fire on the line of the horizon transforming into ash. Then my eyes filled with tears and intense pain wounded my soul. I looked for a shelter to sleep in and took refuge in a small cavity formed between the rocks, almost at the level of the water. As the night wore on, I advanced further inside between the rocks, trying to avoid the darkness, until reaching a point in which the absolute darkness led me to thinking that I had come to the center itself. In the hours that followed, like one who waits all night for something to end, I found contentment. A sudden noise a few moments after concluding this journey did not disappoint me; the water splashed against my feet, along with the morning light; the slow erosion of my body had begun.

—They only gave me the details later on. My hand closed, still searching for a way to cling to life. My face went white as a sheet; my lips turned pale—all this was visible through the death mask. I tried to abstract myself from the individual case. I'm interested in what corresponds to a generalized hypothesis, to apply an apparently unique attitude to the largest number, the diffusion of an individual characters' agony, to remove the drama sustaining humanity.

—And the gaze, still at the beginning of a feeling, but already blind to everything else, is modified in different versions. The changes of meaning are carefully annotated, suffering the evolution due to contact with one's own temporal transformations of vocabulary, making one realize that words are also dying.

—His body fell at his feet. He was reduced to soul, to the whiteness of fire, and only his eyes maintained a material consistency. They were two enormous balls, heavy like life. When they fell, they shattered like glass.

The train was approaching the station. We got up and came closer to the tracks. The Poet's hair was wet.

—On this rainy afternoon, he appeared to me like an unreal figure from a game of transparencies. People played pool in the cafe, there was talk about general useless things: art, politics. I remained silent. A kind of laughter twisted his lips until they finally told me to get out. On our way to the church, the towers stood out as black masses against the night. I loved him; and all that my mind understood of liberty, or of the division of one into two, emerged from his vague fingers and from the profound emptiness of his face.

We began to return.

—In the exasperation of lovers there is no putrefying bulb.

A feeling exists beyond life. But will it be possible to define it? Wood colored eyes intermingle with the earth. I see through the opaque matter of dreams. The cloud's reflection reaches me, the cool wind from the mountains hits me in the face, I hear the cry of an eagle.

Alone, the knight returns to the woods bringing the memory of the beloved dead, and the afternoon shadows darken his face. I drive him to the grave. "Here she is, between the stone and resentment, according to her own desire." In silence, after a lonely moment, a symbolic longing drives him. The return journey takes place with large streams of light and smoke which appear like a fire to the distant observer. Moving in front of him, there was an object in the shape of a cross; it was concave at the ends, radiating bolts of lightning. Fragments of glass and marble slashed the barefoot pilgrims.

I clasped my hand, and a dry noise accompanied the movement of bones and skin. My blood rushed to my head, settling somewhere between my eyes and ears. My lips trembled incessantly and in vain sought to continue the discourse. Words were already destined for another side, and only one last noise of breath reached attentive ears. My body began to cool down. During their last moment of immobility, subterranean animals share their strategies for their final assault. Soon afterwards, I became agitated in quick starts. It was one of those long winter evenings, when the humid moan of the wind entered through the crevices of the compartment, along with the noise of machinery.

—For the first time I picked up a notebook to write down my impressions of life. It was mid-morning and I was in a cafe. I had time. I felt that a change in my nature was taking place. Something inside me was moving around in my head. The disorder of ideas contrasted with the architecture of the cafe. Straight lines, glass, mirrors, marble. I got up and went to the telephone and dialed Clara's number. Nobody answered.

OCTOBER 15

I have her portrait done from memory. We are walking along an empty street at the end of an afternoon. We pass the garden and arrive at the cafe. In the trees, birds prepare for the night. I stay to see her disappear on the stairs of the subway. My eyes invent a mathematical fog.

Today, I can still calculate the number of steps that separated us, the precise meaning of my immobility, the unique way she moved…up until infinity, that is, until we could no longer meet each other, except within a remote sum of divine probabilities.

Elusive hands console me. I drink the waves of the abyss. I am blind because I believe; and the other way around too. I follow a path that was left for me by one who has long given up walking. My footsteps tread on the ancient moss of his tracks. Desolate stars, foreboding twilight—themes to develop.

It is enough for me to see what already seems real to me. The world steams up; yet the horizon is clear like it is after a storm. I have no references—no literature, no history. Emptiness stretches backwards and cannot now begin, since there were already others, precursors to this white presence, who felt it, being furrowed here and there by luminous bodies whose light obfuscates memory, preventing me from recognizing the pale but also fascinating brightness of ephemeral moons.

Seen through the depths of fingers, the sun, vague on the horizon, has the putrid look of marshland converting itself into animal sensation; on the other side, there are oracular depths of past images, voices as clear as transparent eyes or reflections of a vague broken diamond. The blind noise will not reach outside; somewhere in it an outline is sketched, preparing itself for the inevitable future of distant darkness.

One could say that there the relief deepens itself; and the same word that had designated the return, like the black beginning of an absurd course which only unwary mental navigators can follow, leads me to repeat myself in the tenacious isolation of being. Will I get it right so that in this distortion of the irremediable I will return to emerge prepared for the unique solution? I doubt it! And if it does not manifest itself as desire, these sentences have aligned themselves in vain. I will consume myself in a vacuum cleaner for no other purpose than my own demise.

I situate apprehension in a field linked to individual destiny. The worship of another life, parallel to what I introduce here as truth, resembles destiny, the origin of mental mortification. Surprisingly, I only look for the exaltation of being in the exercise of folding pages in half. In a simultaneous game between my composition and its oblivious outline, my confidence invents words in my ear. I look inside myself: a confusion of feelings, the echoes of an initial fall evoke the uneasiness of multiple nights during which, listening to her words, the hours passed until dawn.

The river emerged from the nocturnal fog. I have a vague idea of her darkened face, a darkness in which I lose myself in the depths of memory like a restless soul on the shores of a baleful lake. Still, I hear her talking about love on the dreary eve of memories. "Nothing," I said. And Nothing appears with the evidence of her departure, in the obvious way of revealing a relationship built from

absence. Lucid reasoning, without doubt. A division that pointed to something on the other side, in the obscure synthesis of light and words. Verbal resonant blood…
it is said that the unit, in origin, brought the divine to a calm flow of the fingers over the skin. Life adds nothing to this. But if a brief summary made of a few repeated words explains everything, thought will search in vain to understand the lost initial rule, the source.

I drink to the luck of the cultured navigators of the forbidden browsers. Worlds cross in front of me, reflecting lives on the wall. I stop counting what is only apparently simple. It is not in vain that I stress what was added to me from between sentences. Memory—her portrait! Interior decline of an oval voluptuousness. A movement towards myself. Placed between two possibilities, I headed to the center where an unpleasant sensation infiltrated my thoughts, all in a spiral against the harmony of the spirit, leading me to the formation of a being different from the initial one in which I tried to distinguish myself through observation, as if I were walking amongst the dead.

I met with the Apostate and together we went to visit the Poet. He had not yet recovered. "Two nights without sleep." He continued:

—While others are always talking about me, I'm always talking about myself to others. Is it because they hear themselves in my voice? This perpetual identification between us, this vicious circle is what destroys me, not only on account of my radical refusal to be the person who I am, but because of the potential contact between myself and I, and so on with the others.

The absurdity of my aim was beginning to become evident. I crossed paths with women whose faces I stared at intensely. I chased unrealistic figures who suddenly disappeared forever from a street corner. Longing seized me.

—I no longer recognize people. What I say sounds strange to me. The horizon is suffocating me.

—My tragedy unfolds in the interval between what I say and do.

He puts a cigarette to his mouth with his index finger and his left thumb. He coughs.

—It is from this tragedy that I can obtain the conditions required for creation without interior boundaries. Literature is the destruction of all the possibilities of a personal space under the pressure of the I. Or rather, it is the violent agony of the fingers on the paper during which the paper gets dirtied with paint and blood. While this process lasts, there is a rupture between the writer and the text. Finally, when the brain empties itself and the state of transition to nothing is complete, I find myself again.

He throws away his cigarette and lights another at the same time. My attention is focused on the faces. I walked about randomly, without concentrating my attention on anything concrete. My arms fell. A feeling of inertia.

—Yesterday, at dawn, when Paula sat down in front of me, I prevented myself from touching her. The wind swept the terrace and the sea began to acquire its daytime lividness. For a moment, I had the impression that her silence was going to break. But solitude maintained its dominion.

—On the horizon, the obscure jaws of night vomit out a sick light over the white foam of the rocks.

—The vagueness itself, a noise from somewhere.

I turned myself into a plant, stretched my roots into the earth and sucked the blood that oozed from old walls. The memory of love became non-existent, bodies faint images. Only a virtual quality of being remained, giving me the necessary stimulus to continue living. An impression of eternity was permeating my spirit and was about to lose itself in my soul. I felt vague murmurings that sprouted from the damp lips of the horizon. The desire to arrive increased my anxiety, cutting off my breathing. I approached from the abyss. A well of fog coagulated under me. Suddenly, I felt I was falling, and then I returned to life. I was turning pale; my eyes hurt.

—And love?

—I leafed through my old writings. Reading them left me exhausted, nauseous.

I sought in vain to remember Clara, to reconstitute the warmth of her body. In delirium, I extended my arm and found my skin soaked in sweat. The plaster of the walls became soft, and I sunk my arms into it. My fingers ran up against the cold contours of a body moving under the pressure of a shortness of breath. The Apostate made me sit down.

—It is necessary to rediscover a taste for simple things, the gestures that connect us to life in a material way, freeing us from moral and religious concerns. I still believed in god. However, this god had become a part of myself, living within me in an almost promiscuous intimacy. Sometimes I kiss my image or simply stand in front of a window or a frosted glass to see my reflection. The reflection of the light from my body transports me to another plane of reality in which I feel closer to the true abstraction of real being.

—But you also arrive closer to death.

—But this is not about physical death, rather, connected to the idea of an end to the permanence of the absolute in which everything is reduced.

He had an unhealthy tendency to reconcile opposites. He searched for a point of contact between two different states from which he might ascend to another level of existence, a door that he could deduce from actual existence, but that eluded him in his fleeting encounter with the opacity of his mortality.

—Continue.

—You confuse everything. The garden, Paula?

It was raining. I opened the umbrella. Lightning lit up the sinister faces of the clouds. Initially, nothing was real; but now I was alive, the fusion had begun to take place. The character spoke through my mouth, acted through me without my being able to sketch a movement or gesture.

Both were silent.

—I have been sleeping since the beginning. Things go on in my head but I don't feel them. I simply let them slip into the passive body of history. The way I understand this is based on the conviction that I will advance towards a degree of remoteness from myself that comes down to a single word: unique.

My voice acquired a fragmentary character. The intonation had traces of disease, meaning came to the surface in a residual whisper that remained at the bottom of the mouth.

—Nothing any longer reduces me to being human. I can affirm that as a victory, despite my own temporality: a vague beginning? What I know, I repeat, is that I accompany myself through the zone of shadow in which I wander.

Luminous body radiating light.

—I can sometimes predict the thick liquid agitation preparing the appearance of emotion, but it is not able to penetrate me, nor dare I go towards it, but I stay confined to the space that I occupy without being there.

My suffering came from inside, heavily, from the concave shape of my soul. It involved me as the shell, preventing me from looking at the world; if I were to, the excessive light would force me to return to myself.

—I breath better.

While I was thinking about this, I could not advance in my knowledge of myself or others; on the contrary, my ideas started repeating themselves endlessly. One day I discovered that I was the exact reflection of my own image.

Without being able to get out of it, being aware of being present but still suffering from the void, I was forced to survive through the subterfuge of the word.

—In essence, what is destroying me is the complete impossibility of making myself the subject of my life.

It stopped raining. I remembered those apparently calm days in which, under the trees, I discussed sex and political strategies. Distanced from my heart, hidden and secret, I acquired an almost plant-like existence. I felt alive only when the sun, strained by the motionless leaves, hit me in the tepid coziness of the afternoon.

—At that time, life drowned out both misfortune and happiness. What are we left with? A tired body, looking over itself, yearning for the unparalleled pleasure of death. If somebody tells you that nothing exists, it is because god has corrupted him through love.

—Where then do you find a reason to exist?

—In drowsiness. Here destiny is death. Death restores; hands putrefy. The soul acquires the conviction of nothing.

We arrived. Paula sat between me and the Apostate. We had been drinking wine and aguardente. What I remember is the fruit of abstract and purely visual forms of memory, a few feelings, and the relationships between them and myself, now laying in the midst of the paper. From innumerable fragments I had reached the paroxysm of silence; now I follow a reverse path. I depart from the totality of that which is defined, compact, indivisible. The solidity of the text is what matters. Obstinately, I continue to draw a figure whose metal structure destroys my last illusions of inventing a new vocabulary. My situation is that of a traveler stopped for a moment on the threshold of movement, surprised to see that no road has a beginning.

My indecision produced fruits. Its grainy form corresponded to what I thought: only the gradual destruction of these successive states could arouse contact. If I had thought this from the very beginning, and if my life obeyed a planned strategy, perhaps I would have exorcized the ephemeral and perhaps, even, the subtleties of eternity. But the progression of madness, exposed to the blows of chance, otherwise arranged the relationship between body and soul. Love was not arising from the definitive splendor of moral doubt, but on the contrary, it forced me to return to the original conviction of the circle.

—Lights at the end of the world! The lips on the face in the mirror flashed red in the bedroom. The glass burns away the eczema of your image. There are broken planks in the imprecision of the dream.

—The I is the common point of love.

Paula slipped in beside me. I was choking. I put my hands in my mouth, trying to vomit. I only found a dry hole where the wind infiltrated, making the swollen bellows of my lungs resound hoarsely.

Once again everything slipped through my fingers. In the corner, the Apostate had arisen. He was naked against a background of red curtains. The whiteness of his body stood out violently.

—The only thing that exists is death. What shines is only a state of general transformation. My purity dissipates in contact with the air. The vague voluptuousness of nomadic existence fixes itself in my words, stunning me.

He swung around and fell back on the ground. Paula had left. I stayed under the table, repeating

"I love you" until dawn, trying to remember the last time I kissed Clara: the shadow of her hair partially covered her forehead; her lips were quivering.

—Suddenly I noticed the coldness. I got up to close the compartment window, and when I came back to sit down, she was gone. Could it have been a mere hallucination? The next day I repeated the journey in the same compartment. Nothing.

The leaf of ivy inside the book, the letters closed in a process of inner transformation, the logical arithmetic progression of words from my lips to the sentence, turned my person into something tragic.

—You didn't find her again?

—If I freed myself from the conditional, if not for the use of the imagination, if I had not become distanced from the page and waited there, as in a boat, for the image to free me from her physical presence. I still love her, in perfect vertical suspension. I look for her at home, inside me. Small signs: in the kitchen, a fallen coffee maker, a box of books, letters, torn papers. I can't connect anything. Meaningless fragments.

And I concluded:

—Once I was a globe and there was nothing in my interior which did not concern a spherical form of understanding: conceiving words and actions. But I breathed badly while breathing in a circle. The oscillations of temperament were not conforming to the deep demands of the eternal return. I destroyed myself—as a writing suggestion, as an invulnerable inhabitant of myself. I live in the terror of proliferation, in that which repeats and succeeds, but mostly in that which is multiplied. I need something fixed, a sacrificial obliteration. One where the odor is cloistered.

I reexamine my books. I open them page by page noting the underlined words and phrases, the searches for meaning. I felt trapped in the network of useless relationships and endless games with myself.

—What I'm doing is constantly searching for meaning, for the original source. There is no middle. No interminable lines.

I had decided to stop having a life of my own. Fragments of other beings would feed me. Soon, my words and gestures would coincide with them. Maybe one day the coincidence would be complete and we would find ourselves as one. An outbreak of absolute being. An end.

Already on the train, I saw that the compartments were filled. I stood in the corridor.

It was *La Musica*. Another hypothesis: *The Muse of Icarus*. An abstract novel in a spiral.

There were three of us: Paula, the Poet and myself. We were discussing lunch. The sauce reminded me of certain moments of childhood. Paula wept (the Poet told me afterwards). At the time, I remember having seen her stand up, go to the door and look at length at her own reflection in the glass.

—The water in the lake, she said while sitting down.

The breathing noise suggested autumn. Birds alighted silently on poplars amidst the fog. We hardly knew they existed until one of them fell down dead in front of us.

I was sure it was the last time we would speak of love. The Poet was already suffering from the disturbing thought that war was guiding him towards his destiny. The "exile" or the "bitter desolation of the noun" appeared in his discourse like pieces of a coherent game.

At times, my spirit was absent and I evoked Clara. Her way of laughing, the image of her hands resting on a white towel made me shutter. I felt an absurd need to touch the objects around us, changing their places, arranging them in a new order.

—The purplish circle of the eyes where birds drowned themselves.

—Yes, you could hear the sea beat against the walls of the house; light threatening from outside; and, finally, the rain.

—The past pushed us towards the interior with random phrases, an obscure melancholy, the pallor of an old portrait.

—Paula, how the dried fluids of attics evaporate from your sex like dead wings; and your thighs burn like a fireplace suspended from my blazing fingers!

The Poet continued:

—I see you jumping on the Persian carpet, grabbing a cat by the tail.

The light had been extinguished due to a short circuit. Water symbols melted in my mouth. I say:

—Clara left with me. I crossed the street and waited for Clara on the other side, breathing in the morning's cold air. She was wearing a yellow scarf, and her beret set off blue shimmers in her hair, which from one moment to the next, partially opened me to the hidden world of poetic intuitions. The divisions of physical matter to which her arms were reduced transformed themselves into great elementary spaces, volatile forces imprisoned in the damp cavern of her eyes.

She said:

—Man naturally projects the desires feeding his mind during the day. Women in white dresses, their arms fragmented by the polar lace of rains, the solar communion of sidewalks, all this gets confounded in my imagination with the possibility of a stable relationship of which I count on the scattered words that intimacy leads me to formulate.

At the incubus level of consciousness, a dual nature reconciled me with the hot sun of childhood.

—I forgot to bring the books.

I studied philosophy. The Greeks, the Gnostics. The androgynous appeared to me on the horizon as multiple projections of Clara's pale face. I interspersed leaves and wilted petals while randomly opening the pages. I touched their lips to assure myself of an osmosis between the human and vegetable. She said to me: "The soul is in the interior of one's being and not the contrary."

I didn't expect anyone on the other side. I had often been given to understand that I would be indifferent to hearing her speak, but the systematic silence was beginning to become unbearable. I still lived with her image in front of me, maintaining the ironic smile with which she used to bid people farewell. We had a relationship based on our shared cruelty towards ordinary beings, beings whom we thought to be ordinary at that time. Many disappeared into obscure provincial life: lawyers, teachers, or employees in public offices; and there were those who vanished suddenly, about whom we learned sometime afterwards that they had gone to war in Africa. It was better, then, not to think about these things. I took her hands, we drank coffee and aguardente and laughed at the Poet who, at another table, filled up long sheets of paper with great thoroughness.

Poetry had a decorative function in this cocoon-like existence in which we sought to deceive ourselves. I'd brought books of English poetry with me which I read with difficulty. Rarely can I read a poem to the end. The idea of death interposes itself between me and the words, and I get stuck in a dark knot of primitive emotions. To free myself from this inexplicable state, I need music. With her this didn't happen: neither music nor poetry. I was in the presence of the Poet, listening to his vague speeches. His theory dragged us into night wanderings along the river. We ended up in the company of the last drunks of the city.

One afternoon, a madman sat down in front of me. He began to explain a confusing story in which the sound of bells mingled with an indecipherable family problem. I realized that he needed my help to make a phone call. I agreed to help him and followed him to a phone booth. The phone didn't work. He became desperate. With an obstinate murmur, he shook his head and brought his hands to his eyes. I noticed then that he had a tumor in the place of one of his ears. It was a ball of flesh with bloody veins. Two flies had gotten stuck in the scabs where they languished.

The Poet called me. I left the madman and went down to the river. Paula tried to stop me. The twilight wind pushed the autumn clouds to the south towards the sea. When I turned around, the Poet was sitting there, staring fixedly at the ground.

—Clara?

There was no reply. The amorous dialogue could contain the unhappy multiplicity of our voices. In this confluence, the angel acquired solar scintillations; dawn exuded the luminous fragrance of communicable cabinets.

The restaurant was going to close. At the pier we found the Apostate who had lost his lower belly in an odor of citations, and we took the primordial boat of the trinity.

—The worst was when I touched the wound, the warm scar, said the Apostate, as the boat pulled away from the shore.

—Yes, Paula cried. A bloody bird was agitated under her pubis, entangled in the mnemonic mesh of the shoreline. Clara cried from the spiral stairs:

—What do you want from me?

The slow movements in the cemetery resembled the draining of fluids. Syntactic choreography. The murmur of incestuous relationships (in my opinion). Everything could be summed up as a concept of ethics:

—Systematic abstention ought to regulate physical contacts.

Platonic proposal. Her naked shoulders revealed to me the credibility of desire (I would have preferred the imaginary connection, love subjected to the mandatory distance of looks).

Paula separated herself from the imprecise tangle of the pier and stood there, hung by my coat on an iron hook.

—What logic? Dialogue of improbable shadows?

Exhausted, I amplify the images. The day is extended by the difficulty in apprehending the simplest of things; the natural light turns off, but the irradiated glow of bodies is sufficient. The image of her breasts that I released from her blouse survives in that light as a lamentation bearing my nostalgia for the infinite. She stands against the grey horizon of my memory; her beak emerges from the arid whiteness of her fingers and acquires the configuration of the very idea of a sensitive target, subject and symbol.

—Have you ever undressed her?

I said:

—She is still a virgin.

The answer was given according to my own (stunted) moral order. The Apostate laughed. He still had Paula's sex in his mouth, the tiny vowel, the acidic pearls of urine.

—I see the naked light of the end, the imprecise line of dusk emerging from the limits of ethics.

I am beginning to take shape. I acquire qualities: an opaque body, speech—and from my lips all my future opportunities sprout out whole.

—But I no longer know who I am. I am lacking a name. I return to my origin in the exact place where genealogies are lost, confused in the mist of the ages. And if I had a generation? If before me came others who only lacked taking shape just like me? Depending on me to be realized?

I still do not completely exist, and I already torment myself with the superfluous.

—That is, I say that life is nothing else but this very movement in which being is continuously spent between the excessive and the unnecessary.

Then I conclude: to return to the beginning, and, thus, to being (non-being)?

—Everything is equal; it only hurts me to know that the difference exists somewhere beyond me, and

I am not able to reach it! I can see it on the horizon, as the ghost of the oblique sail to the Antipodes.

—No. It is best to be nothing. Definitively: nothing.

—Yes, life tires me. But the return to the imagination, the dream, the escape from myself, steals sleep, torments me, gives me fevers, and I find myself sitting, without strength, staring at an abstract point on the wall. I stay that way for hours, waiting for the sky to fall on me or (which is the same thing) not expecting anything. Painfully I criticize this existential sloppiness. I get up suddenly and drink a coffee, cross the street, buy a newspaper. It is all useless. I return to the emptiness, to the obscure nothingness of thought. And I have nothing to say. The time for justifications has passed, my rhetoric does not provide the vague sincerity of remorse. Only music diverts me, for a moment, from immobility. I create an artificial exaltation, a spasm of memory between baroque reflections of a sonorous light. Will it be in this that I wear myself out? That I slowly lose the last desire to exist? Even if the twilight were to bring me its dead laughter, or if the trees whispered the lost name along lonely boulevards…

—I said: "I love you."

"A point of passage," she answered.

Perceptions of reality pass through a double mirror image with three meanings: the practical, the metaphysical and the phantasmagorical. The first dislocates reality, the second completes it and the third turns it into an object of desire. As if I was in perfect complicity with the text, my transgression magically formulates it. Water boils in the kettle. I pour the jasmine tea into a cup. It has yellow and green reflections around the rim. I breath in the infusion, the cosmic brotherhood, the dirt road towards the cove, the blueish slope, the eastern waterline converted into watercolors. The image was taking shape. Remorse, inside of me, the white house, the intervals between people in a photo layout, faces long unseen. I predict the amazement, the future unrest, memories—they were coming from the most remote places of the past, where the murmur of lines sweetens the tone until everything in childhood is reduced to vague orders, smells, and acid light. Knowledge of its corners makes the house appear much smaller. I undo the enchantment of distance, the close proximity of landscapes, life in the regularity of its seasons. Time passes rapidly, moving us closer to the approach of the dark age when one day I wake up and that's it, it's done, time will have already decisively ruined me. Is it not worth shedding tears over the salty river, the brand of your machine? The fingers of the woman I loved between February and June of a given year? Or should I say October? Or even today? The image pursues me now, much clearer and faster, the golden moments flow, dispersed by the currents of wind and sea. After concluding this reflection, I know it is all so pointless, the infinite, the mirrored image, the projection on the wall, the poor condition of the film, the hoarse voice translating the subtitles, the pointer on the board. You should not use the gerund or gerundive. The best tenses are the active ones, nothing of dead tenses, interior orientations, paths of rhetoric among flowers, the lucid spring. Whose voice survives. January. 1970, zwei Monde des Uranus Leipzig, winter semester. Windows. Wind. Sleep. The circulation of the worlds of which I am still the center, the copula, my companions, seagulls and crows on the overhanging cliff howling by the lighthouse under the reflections I see things through a thick fog noticing afterwards that I have dirty glasses, I clean them, attach a gummed label to the breakfast mass bread the Lord abundant vomit mutilated members eyes the inexpressible lower lip of god's eardrums a sexual organ

I meditate attentively in astonishment on existence
I dissolve a great lozenge in my mouth the red box
clock seven to ten days in the cup the tea an already
cold dark liquid made in England I go outside to use
the telephone on the wall it was already night I looked
at the ground excrement vomit urine stains 66 what
you want is 69 I sit down at a table in the café by the
window there are papers yellowed by the sun I open
the book that I brought with me in the gardens big
viscous masses diverse shades of brown next to tufts
of trees and shrubs shaped like black dog shit in cylin-
drical forms along the sidewalks amidst flower beds
beside the legs of tables in the esplanades at dawn
torn newspapers exceptional weather conditions with
neither rain nor wind generally the stain of excrement
was near the folded pages with advertisements necro-
logical news printed crosses sacrilegiously sometimes
stained the deceased's face concealing the vomit I get
to the highway and request a ride a couple in a Taunus
take me to the airport I establish a hierarchy of vomit
beans and the most common red wine or breakfast
the undigested mass of coffee with milk and bread
the dirty vans the smell of hastily washed upholstery
the leather worn out by the heat of the August voy-
ages paint the white face the body without strength
will come to take me at exactly midnight new year's
eve the noise of water the sawdust public urinals wet
papers exterior stairs of dimly lit buildings backsides
of churches thresholds of buildings designated for

demolition shades of grey and yellow in the corners
the oldest darkest layer often already mildewed or
with a layer of dust near the door, the light, an almost
pure yellow the acidic smell permeates the walls and
the doors the message descended upon me, on the
ground, lying in the sun that warms me, an ordinary
sun that masturbates me, I force myself to visit the
taverns on the pier buying myself glasses of wine and
stretching out on the benches in front of the station,
listening to the panting of the machines.

   This is a screen in which the weight of the line
breaks the margin an excess of earth forces the foot to
dig itself in the direction of the senile center therefore
it is an act against people technical power action break
down the wall he writes be read before they come
to impose we would say to ourselves erroneously he
wished his body would accompany him in the ascent
of his soul but he cut it down with a single blow and
left it creating roots Here is a place where no one will
ever endure the smell of rotten flesh contaminating
words that force the lips to space out each syllable
until the limits of the comprehensible These sounds
that suspend sleep resurge in dreams the Sibilant
wind the single syllable in a simple consonant the
whisper vanishes in a puff of salt. I was thinking about
the death of the world where the dream has a definite
logic. I call you. A swarm of flames. It rains. It was
nothing. The interior ceilings bloomed in my head,
and I stood open like a fruit whose juice is spilt. My

knee hurt me. The sea was filling up with strange cargo ships I already sang the sea a coastline of seagulls the twilight correspondence of cliffs I walked in silence along the pale decks of stars I loved the agonizing life of a dream of summits the barred gates opened themselves when I approached and drank the wine of the dead under the gloomy domes of the ultimate celebration sleep sound self.

Spend your best New Year's Eve ever
in the select ambience of the famous "CAVE"
which presents our exclusive band

THE GODS

MENU

Creme of Tomato
Fisherman's Style Clams
Stuffed Turkey
Fruit
Dessert
Coffee
Brandy
A Bottle of Champagne s/4 People

Choose from three options:

Dinner with access to the "CAVE" *180 €00*
Dinner without access *80 €00*
Drinks in the nightclub *100 €00*

On the stage, standing under a tall screen, a man sang: "I don't want any of that/smoked sausage/or swiss mountain cheese/under a spider's web/crazy ideas you have in your head!/I don't want any of those/potatoes in seaweed/novalis or chamisso/cock or dick/well cooked and thick/I don't want any of that." A pale young man sits in front of me. He has Clara's face. The pain remains. The spoils of love stay in my mouth. His face stares out into a succession of images. I turn to an old photograph found among the "Trophies." Amidst strangers her eyes keep the inaccessible knowledge of the future intact. Like a "noise" that deafens me to the present, voices interrupt her presence inside me, cutting off the opportunity of conserving myself in her name. Yet my own voice reflects her, bends itself before her, what I express runs in her direction as an inverted watercourse, I split myself between impulses that self-divide and lacerate. I am pieces, fragments, parts that putrefy in the extreme division of this body. I use her as a unifying point from a previous past that I didn't live through. Without reconciling myself, she makes me momentarily coincide with myself. I insist meanwhile that it's only the images that I've created as a unique self in appearance that still enable the course of my existence to be continuous. And if this effort at understanding myself within this tenuous limit of a physical border definitively distances me from the possibility of having a soul, it's not because of that that I'm closer to having a material existence. To love her? Here inside. I am in the heart of the text. My fingers are filled with mud, the entrails of time open themselves to the naked eye. I remember. My lips whisper incessant music, something that changes, transforming the fluid obstacles of rhythm into opaque constructions, tributaries of the image, noises, metaphors of lead. The horizon is loaded with rain, greyness that memory fixes into sickly autumn shadows in the finishing of the sentence, the moment that arises in the verticality of the dream and converts itself into movement. I turn backwards, the discovery of the poetic step on the page reproduces the emotion. All that it repeats about nothing attaches and detaches itself from me, eventually leaving behind, just before the end, the gesture of a writer.

He tells me that the fire of the afternoon spreads to the brain. But I saw his eyes open a grey dawn, corrupting the disintegrating mist. A whiteness of hands emerged from within me. I follow him in a delirium of sunken boats. I know I'll get somewhere under the protection of the dead, and yet my fingers hesitate to touch him. Distance began in a progression of words. Luminous volumes accumulated in front of me. I am alone in a movement of vague musical falling. Sometimes it appeared to me that I was looking down from the belly of big birds. Suspended, I saw land in the fluid transparency of clouds. When I found him again in the undefined pallor of the day, he was motionless.

A bird-like silence agitated him, the smile of death had landed on his lips. The resolution of a puddle in the solitude of god. Smooth inebriation of love, hardened shell of the soul that time erodes, a circle closed upon the indecipherable end, in the con-torted navel of the horizon, the movement of acids in the necropolis of phrases, in the opened eyes the insoluble asphyxiation of the shadow, a whipping of horses in the fixation of madness, a red cup of drib-ble, green foams of the labyrinth transforming the architecture of blind delirium, pain scattered in crys-tals of sound transfigured by reason. What is dead, however, still irrigates the nascent human breathing. A tomb of wings between spheres and numbers faces the ruined beauty.

8

Grey clouds began to fill the sky. Waves, whose peaks were blackened by erosion, emerged on the surface, swelling like large living muscles, bursting against the rocks. Despite this, I continued in the direction of the estuary. A vast surface composed of a cluster of contrasts stretched out in front of me as far as the eye could see, and now my gaze fastened onto a clearer tone until my vision, in sudden metamorphosis, darkened. I looked for a rarer shade of grey, somewhere on the horizon, covered by foam, dragged in by the wind. The sky and sea formed a violent contrast to the beach, both by the nature of their elements, and by their inherent thickness. And the surface of the sea, adjacent to the ancient security and material of the beach, came into opposition with a sky now darkened, now more clear, in continuous transformation and overloaded in all its extensions by the clouds that moved towards the south, where figures of birds flew about unflinchingly facing the storm in their static whiteness.

—One day I came to this same place, alone. On the sand, in low tide, small ponds formed, and hundreds of seagulls landed in compact flocks. As I approached, they began to take flight. At the same time, I saw two naked girls who were swimming in one of these pools and who, upon noticing my presence, fled to the opposite bank. Since then, I've associated seagulls with flocks of naked girls, taking flight at my approach with frantic screams that echo from the horizon.

It was concerning this impression that the idea came to me to write an aesthetics of landscape whose principles would be based on the description of an object from within me, in which the descriptive tone would not be subject to objective requirements. After identifying an indefinite number of contours and variations of shapes, surfaces, volumes, lines, colors, shades, environments, climates, and atmospheres, I obeyed my choice to pursue an unlimited subject, such as the sea, to the extent that it was possible; but in the circumstances that I described, this was only a way to escape from myself.

—Your body lay in the sea, immovable, suggesting a marsh of magnolias.

I was beginning to think that words, when a new sense touches them, differentiate themselves by forming a more human dimension. This idea became an obsession. I intended to extend myself into my writing, although I couldn't stop thinking of a way of transforming my own life in terms that would ultimately form a coherent whole from which I could produce a "philosophical treatise" or something of that nature.

And I returned to the initial sentence. I said it because the image of Clara came to my mind unexpectedly. Once said, it constituted a reflective act in which I could see myself intact and united though not forming more than a general and confusing appearance of an interior whole.

—I represent.

Under the ambiguous gesture of an actor, her sharp gaze was revealed to me while I continued to maintain the ambivalence of being solitary.

—All these abstractions taken in themselves are disconnected from objective reality, and having no value, can only serve to qualify the initial stratification of the logical path. Once these qualities have been exhausted, reality replaces words altogether, despite having made possible the objective conditions of speech.

The earth darkened with the arrival of dusk. In the stagnant course of the river a glow reflected the last light from the horizon. In the general silence, birds suddenly sought the shelter of the dunes. My eyes crossed with the blind eyes of a dead girl. My fingers touched the swollen skin, and I inhaled her decomposed breath along with the violent smell of coastal plants.

I began walking faster, trying to catch the last afternoon train. I wasn't able to. I stood still, as if I had suddenly become consciously aware that reality had divided itself into two apparently equal but essentially contradictory parts.

—Reality isn't real, but everything real fits into reality. Bent under the weight of the real without being able to look up, man cannot free himself from his interior horizon. While he is reflected in that impression of being real, he is transformed into an image of himself that soon disappears, fading into the vague restriction of nothingness. That is why I reaffirm the identity of this very real divide. Nothing will keep me from the conviction that before myself, I am not other than myself. The two forms that I assume, although contradictory, faithfully reflect my divided identity. Following this, I divide the sentence, and the body within the sentence, so that being fragmented and diverse, I can analyze my decomposition, somewhere between the reality of the body and the body of reality.

One day I was able to have this impression, or its pale reflection. It was a grey day. The sea in front of the hotel was filling up with white flakes. The wind beat down on my body. It was then that I became aware that time had a physical existence in an order of reality separate from my own.

—The impression that I had of these days is one of a complete void filled with intense consciousness of this void—even then I could feel the diffuse divinity announced by the wind and breath through it, such as when climbing a snow covered peak where the vision of the sun beating against the cliffs reaches the soul.

From the sea, the contrast between the dull grey sky and the luminous backs of birds heading for earth was accentuated. Space is a void that the soul fills with difficulty, along with the love of the mountains and the wilderness, a vague notion that the human spirit is not accustomed to. But there are times when one is next to the sea, when one feels that thought doesn't fit the image and that this, in itself alone, combines nothingness with the divine. In this case, days spent in contemplation of the horizon allow for the creation of a philosophy of the very physical form of being, winding along coastal cliffs with the hesitant and unaccustomed step of one who begins the arduous path of winter.

I had already passed the small lagoon, harrowed by the wind of twilight. The noise of the sea reached me from afar, muffled by the sultry moan of the bushes. I walked inland towards the tavern whose isolated light was evident in the dark. Behind me were ancient caves ripped into the deep rock by the crashing sea.

—I travel along the vast white coastline of the paper.

I outline the precise margins and the exact contours of a transitional vocabulary that the sea itself would submerge in the great semantic tides of the future.

—I remember a poem I'd written about the sea. My impulse came from an attempt to define the word—sea, as a vast and immense abyss, which by itself is the sole element of water, extending its infinite arms, receiving in its fingertips the tribute of all the rivers of the universe. However, in this first definition, confusion arose between the sea and the ocean; thus, I distinguished between what was formerly called "the sea," or *mare magnum*, and which is only the Mediterranean, from the ocean itself, which is what is simply called the sea to signify the expanse of water that occupies a part of the globe, in opposition to the earth. The result would be a vast extension of the poem, occupying the greater part of the page and pouring itself over the blank margins in large threatening waves of vocabulary. The table resembled a stormy sky, threatening rain, the blackening soul and the poem.

Dark colors. Hidden moon. Sensation of disgrace. Lips move noiselessly over these impressions. I murmur that nothing has to do with me. I move obsessively towards the light. As a result of having become conscious, I'm beginning to find out that nothing exists. What I feel resembles a sudden hole in the reflux of despair. Will I know if life is being irretrievably and increasingly lost from day to day?

—Nature? A virtue—your reflection in the frosted glass window between the leaves.

Life suddenly deviates from this framework. It remains a landscape of sand, the sea in the distance, a low suffocating sky, twilight at the end of the world. I sit down. I'm beginning to see the sea: a large surface of water with density, volume, unsheltered and tempestuous. Then there are squares, insulas, lands, capes, promontories, sandbanks, coastlines, uniformity, without relief, giving access to new shores at the extremity of the horizon. From its evaporation in the warm seas, Water—in vast non-uniform extension—collides within itself at all levels of depth, now forming large blue glaciers or suddenly drifting off or covering the imagination with sweeping scabs of swans.

My initial intention would have been to exalt natural values—the storm, the wind of the square, the breath of the great western caves—to free myself from terrestrial limitations. It was a mystical operation. From where I stood, I could see the ships that crossed the horizon. Some quickly disappeared, leaving the entire hemisphere suddenly empty; but others followed the line of the horizon, following the curvature of the Earth, moments before disappearing into an oblique spasm. Thus, a space for reflection was created in which one could distinguish fragments of space, spots of color, aerial vibrations, up until the limits of the imagination. With the sunrise, however, a thick humidity erases all of these phenomena, and the fog closes its gaze in inner contemplation in the invention of unique and mysterious landscapes, inaccessible to language.

—She was in front of me, her hair falling onto her shoulders; her face had the tone of marble, and yet blood ran in her veins, her eyes stared into me with bitter distance, her hands were like fruits resting at the rosy end of spring.

I got up. Rain had begun to fall; the afternoon came to an end. Her image perturbed me. I was beginning to realize what was broken and dead inside me.

I took shelter in the tavern.

—When there is bad weather, sea birds usually land on the dunes, in the bushes, along the harbors of coastal inlets, or on the grand sandbanks of the estuary. The sea has a grey color, the waves break along the cliffs in large white explosions. The low and heavy clouds are immobilized at the edge of the horizon, transmitting a feeling of faint anguish reflected by the depths of memory in various shades of white and grey on the paper. Loneliness is conjured up in the diurnal metamorphosis of the body. The gaze receives the quality of the center, outlining the indefinable contours of the soul.

On the counter, an oil lamp had cast a wandering light, reflected in dirty tones in the glass bottles.

—By analogy, I continued, I create the image of a ship subject to storm. It doesn't manage to find the shelter of a port or protected coast. It is certainly going to be wrecked. It is beaten by the great northern winds moving, like a little bird, following the waves without aim, stability or weight.

The remote grey design of the eyelids. The contrast between the undecided color of the hands and their precise position closed on the table in an attitude of expectation—a passage to somewhere else where there is a clear opening, the exact perspective of transformation.

I went up to the attic. The wind howled in the house beneath me, and this howl came to me muffled by the thick lining of the ceiling. The storm hit in successive gusts against the roof. I stretched out on the floor in the dust amidst old carpets and packs of torn letters. Through the open cracks between broken tiles I saw lightning illuminate the deluge. I decided to go downstairs to the terrace. Electricity came and went. The lights of the deserted rooms went on and off in an incoherent sequence of intermittent light. When I opened the door of the terrace facing the sea, the wind thrust water into the house. It covered me: rain, foam, the cry of a wounded animal amidst clouds. Then there was calm, and then it was possible to see a downpour of water falling regularly from the eaves. I sat back down on the floor, receiving solicitations over my body from outside, an obscure calling from the storm, the conscience of which the dry and clean world had definitively terminated at the end of the night with that livid and humid light that corrupted my eyes and hands.

(?)

"I'm here smoking a Pall Mall and thinking of shaving my beard (which I did). I'm lying in bed letting time pass. The light passes through the shutters and soaks my legs. I dry off during the night. Bedbugs bite my armpits.—A crazy painter, a misanthrope…someone said while looking at the photograph. Very close up: a protagonist from hell. To me he said: what I demand of myself, currently, is non-literary literature. And: the novel is, for now, shrapnels of prose."

NOVEMBER 3

Four in the morning: Rachel, the vicious one, appeared in a Renault 8 with a yoga practitioner, a Basque and an imbecile.

(Discrete) requirement: to provide clear evidence of bisexuality in *jumping*. The Apostate, effusive as ever, silver-haired, bright with unexpected obscenity, aired his sex on the hood of the car.

I admire the perfection of the season. The end of the time for solitary games: the solitude played in groups. Variations of the *voyeur* in bed.

NOVEMBER 8

I continued to pass my days in bed. I do nothing. Yesterday, however, I resolved to go outside. I read the newspaper all afternoon. I memorized three or four articles. An automobile accident: four deaths. A war. Disaster. Afterwards, I entered the tobacco shop, briefly leafed through the books, went to the square along the river, smoked.

I establish a rule: to flee from those who know me. To increasingly write less. James Keiller & Son Ltd Established 1797 Original Dundee—Grapefruit Marmalade—Made with sugar syrup grapefruit. Bad poems. (The circle that his hand so subtly draws, begins and ends in its own circle.)

DECEMBER (?)

(About the characters:) they appeared out of nothing. Their material bodies, suddenly appear animated—then discouraged. The old conviction was lost, or rather, transformed into something that nobody makes an effort to fix. But it is already too late. Also, they know that they stand at the frontier between one and another limit, under the gaze of everyone, shadows fading into the twilight.

DECEMBER

Love is an interruption from being. The relationship dissipates in the interval between bodies. Rachel turned off the radio and said to me: "the skin of women, the occult moon." The following day I caught the train. Two days traveling; cramps in my soul. When I arrived, I checked myself into a hotel and took my temperature. I was sick. At dawn I vomited on the stairs. An employee came out of a closet in the hallway holding an electric flashlight. The wallpaper glistened with the red reflection of purgatory. I extended my arms to the sword of a flaming angel; his feathers were torn by X-rays indicating tuberculosis, the bird cough, the Syrian, the protector. I crawled inside; the photograph of Rachel came from inside the bag. The fornicator of vaginas was laughing at my sick eyes. I took a fried egg from her mouth. She turned around to the other side and continued to sleep. I turned on the light. Neon rays trembled. I read her the short biographical note over a weak broken flame. Ruins. Fever. Narrative pain. I hear the screams of bloody fig trees. The wall opens cracks. The noise of the rose. Gardens ruined by fierce climbing plants. Legs torn with nails. Shoulders bitten by the inner serpent. Orpheus scares the margins, drives women mad with the memory of an ancient feast.

DECEMBER (CONT.)

Winter celebrated between sheets of sludge. The agonizing breath in the fingers of words on the horizon. A groove of light corrupts the drowned body. The level of the gaze rises with the depth of movement towards the "inside" of oneself.—How that points to the plunge!—The interior female composition imprints itself in purple lips. A circle of birds parallel to the concentric circle of water under the bridge. The light of flames at the center of the fleeting night.

Once born, she spread disappointment among those who've waited for her. Announcer of absences. Cities of blue stone.

(20 MINUTES TO 5 IN THE AFTERNOON,
FEBRUARY 3, 1969)

"What about lunch and the cold lunch recipe?
    I have no words,
because the game of freedom is not the yoke—
the guests—who are they?
Who is the tomato sauce for?—If it was blood the lunch
would be hot and the gypsies would eat it
    now there is only my non-voice."

(MINUTES LATER)

"The gypsy holds your card, outraged by god and man.

Frustration is where metaphysics is created.

Now I observe the signs of men in the stars and in the roads.

What is the word before the eyes?

The gypsy's hands are exhausted from all the music, only my fingernails have life, and now they are destroyed.

The Revolution is absolutely necessary.

Long live the Revolution and all the eyes and hands that know how to tear up the free pathways in the midst of the game."

(YEARS LATER)

Inert life. Memory removed from the hyalograph. The clear sky. The Assumption. The brusque silence of the boat. Summary. The scar of the beloved matrix. A twilight infected by small laurifolios, red-haired insects. The celibate brain in front of the bookcase— the exposed sex organ deflowers a book.

Summary: in the distance, at the end of the afternoon, the ruined walls of the convent, a bell rings for ambushed highwaymen whose memory vanishes on the stage of nocturnal threshing floors. The moon swells in the purple sky. I tread the earth thinking about the bodies that it shuts in. Broken bones emerge on the surface, carpus, metacarpus, pericarps stick to my feet. A waviness roughened the rooftops.

(Continue in this sequence) the sick images are accumulated in the room. I smell like vomit and excrement. A dog enters, lies down on the hole-ridden carpet. I discover a bucket filled with a dead person's putrid urine under the bed.

(Reduction of the body to the dimension of an egg.)

The formal process feeds the funereal mouth. Cold slugs descend from the humid wall, climbing up my arms, making their way to my neck. Fever exalts me—my soul—closes itself.

—The reason? But how to reconcile myself with my wounded soul, consuming desolate images? Pleasure is only associated with transitory conditions. Ideas of despair escape from the casual augury of death, symbols of the sun. It appears that life stops; the night, then, represents the only hope of the open lips, sonorous like the storm at the summit of the mountain.

I unfold the sheet stained with blood and malignant puss and dip my own hands into the fetid liquid and put them to my lips, drinking, as if from an anointed bowl. The bread and wine of the flesh; food that dripped from the heart that had drained itself through infected wounds that was now returning to the beginning.

(A RAINY DAY IN SPRING)

I dreamed about the birth of a vowel at the center of the word. The strange sound of interior music drove my lips to pronounce it, confining me to the margin of the pronoun; and, while I looked for a luminous opening in the dark shell of the sentence, I arrived at the bottom of my essential vision. A song of praise subtracting the meaning from the sleepy inquietude of the figure. Remote, almost dead, exuding a suggestion of verbal rites. Body placed in the arena of language—vague insect.

(AND I CONCLUDE:)

I have taken into account my inner state.

I dwell (the verb is used in the exact sense—for depth, the well) inside myself, in the darkness surrounding the core of what I consider my "soul," where I encounter a negative illumination.

I call it the impulse or desire for nothing. I oppose creative intuition with a religious form of facing myself, but with such fragility that it causes me to pass through several states in which matter and spirit alternate.

I feel myself descending in the direction of the original liquid, between fish and traces of invertebrates, but I'm still stuck in a "heavy" world.

Shall I relinquish my conscience?

It's not just the artificial heat of fever that makes me different from the inert internal universe; it's also the gaze, which while giving me the image of an external thickness and opacity, fastens me to myself, preventing me from definitively disconnecting myself from who I am.

I can, however, close my eyes. But the noises, the cold, the fragmentary life… Thus, I end up writing. And it is this suspension of myself that, sometimes, I give up (I un-exist).

Here is an idea: "the construction of total death."
The voice appears without me even intuiting it; it's
useless for me to try to master it, to hear it, limiting
it to what I have to say.

(AT THE SAME TIME)

I frequently fall asleep over a page. My face merges
with the paper. I go down a white well, quietly, where
I cease to have something to say; and painfully, I feel
the awakening, the return to the normal world of sensation and vocabulary.

One day was different: I was in a big house without furniture, with a façade that opened out onto a
deserted square: old buildings, abandoned wagons,
dry trees. I closed the window. The apocalypse
machine was moving.

*Small boats anchored in the cove. Bright colors, blue,
red. Swollen boats on land with their bellies turned up
like putrefying whales. The marginal dirt road, poor
houses, roofs with patches, under naked hills, dried trees,
charred shrubs. The full midsummer sun's shadows lurk
close to my feet. I lift my leg and they emerge. Timidly,
I take a step and they disappear, only to re-emerge. I get
used to staring at the ground. Grains of earth, remains
of shells, sand. I sit on the step that leads to a dark stone
beach. Intense heat. The seagulls fly in a circle, silently,
slowly. Mountain tops. I'm sitting on a wooden chair.
I cut my hair in the morning. I read magazines. I listen
to the flies in the room. Ordinary desks. I smell bags of*

grain. I hear a glass drop in the warehouse. Laughter. The muffled sound of automobile noises. I can't get up. I hear the clock. The slowness of hands. It's the early afternoon. "There were small boats anchored in the cove," one of the employees told me. "The storm threw everything onto the beach." But here there are no storms. The interiors of the rooms have a uniform temperature; only once in a while, a vague wind enters through the crevices above. Reminiscences of the field. I let smoke pass through my mouth. Gloves. Purple fingers. I begin to run. The path forks: to the farm, the forbidden place of marshes and reeds, and to the train tracks, the bridge, the gap between.

—"Everything was thrown onto the beach," he repeats. But I remember the buried boat. At low tide the tip of the bow is still visible, the wood eaten away by salt. I lay behind it, and it formed the center of the world. An invisible compass drew the semicircle of the horizon and stopped at both ends of the earth: on the right side of the lighthouse at the tip of the cape, on the left side of the rocks, ochre, green patches. Flat landscape.

—We're about to close.

I get up. Now the shadows are big. I don't feel the heat. The birds have disappeared. The street remains deserted, the doors and the wooden window shutters are closed. Sometimes, a buzzing insect passes through the air. I turn to look at the ground in search of tunnels opened by ants last spring. Shadows hide everything.

Translating Nothing

WHEN I BEGAN TRANSLATING *A MANTA RELIGIOSA* I knew very little Portuguese and had no idea what it was about. In my first draft I wrote down what I thought was going on. I looked up words and phrases, but mainly I tried to imagine what it might sound like in English, the flow, the intensity. What inspired me was the way it looked inwards at the making of poetry and the identity or non-identity of the author. Most of all, it seemed to be about the making of something out of nothing, only this something was none other than the nothing out of which it was being made. In the words of Nuno Júdice in *A Manta Religiosa*, "poetry is nothing".

Mantis religiosa refers to what we call in English a praying mantis and in Portuguese *louva-a-deus* or *louva-deus*. The cover of my translated edition includes a photograph of my painting "Sermon on the Mound." My painting connects to the theme of poetry as religiosity and shows how the poet's hands translate thoughts into art, and how the teacher and disciple, author and reader, just like the poet and his multiplicities, are ultimately the same person.

—*DAVID SWARTZ*

NUNO JÚDICE (Mexilhoeira Grande, 29 April 1949) is an essayist, poet, writer, novelist and professor.

Poet and fiction writer, his first poetry book was published in 1972. He graduated in Romance Philology from the University of Lisbon and obtained the degree of Doctor from the New University of Lisbon (Universidade Nova), where he was professor until 2015. He received Spain's Queen Sofia Ibero-American Poetry Prize in 2013, awarded by the Spanish National Heritage and the University of Salamanca. He was the commissioner for the area of Literature "Portugal as a country-theme" in the 49th Frankfurt Book Fair. In 1996, he released the poetry magazine Tabacaria, edited by "Casa Fernando Pessoa" until 1998. In 1997, he was appointed Cultural Counselor of the Embassy of Portugal and Director of the Camões Institute in Paris. In 2009, he assumed the direction of Colóquio/Letras, the literary magazine of the Gulbenkian Foundation. He has works translated in Spain, Italy, Mexico, France, where he published *Un chant dans l'épaisseur du temps* in the Collection Poésie chez Éditions Gallimard. He translated poetry and theater of such authors as Emily Dickinson, Pablo Neruda, Molière, Shakespeare. He is curator for the cultural area José Saramago Foundation, created in 2008.

Originally from Toronto, Canada, **DAVID SWARTZ** has resided in Lisbon, Portugal since 2013, where he teaches English at the Universidade Nova de Lisboa. Some of David's recent translations include Nuno Júdice's "An essay on inspiration" (Berkeley Poetry Review, Issue 46, 2016), *And Painting: Questioning Contemporary Painting*, CIEBA-FBAUL, 2016), and *Matteo Lost His Job* by Gonçalo M. Tavares (Absinthe 21: 2015). In collaboration with New Meridian Arts, David is preparing a translation of *Orpheu – Triannual Literary Journal, Volumes 1 and 2* (1915).